MONSTROUS GRAVE

Monstrous Grave
Copyright © 2024 by Rainelyn

Rainelyn asserts the moral right to be identified as the author of this work.

All rights reserved. This is a work of fiction. Names, characters, places, events and incidents either are the product of the author's imagination or are used fictitiously. Any similarities to real persons, living or dead, events or places, is coincidental and not intended by the author.

All brand names and product names used in this book are trademarks, registered trademarks, or trade names of their respective holders. Sourcebooks is not associated with any product or vendor in this book.

No portion of this book may be reproduced, or stored in a retrieval system, or transmitted in any form or by any means, electronic, mechanical, photocopying, or otherwise, without express written permission of the publisher.

ISBN: 978-91-527-7571-4

Cover design by: Rainelyn
Formating by: Rainelyn
Editing by: Rumi Khan
Proofreading: Lindsey Clarke

MONSTROUS GRAVE

RAINELYN

*For the good girls who want to be corrupted by a masked biker,
kidnapped and hunted through the woods, and then fucked by a gun.
This sociopath is waiting for you*

PLAYLIST

Tell Me The Truth || Two Feet

Nightmares || Two Feet

Washed Away || Savage Hands

Patterns || Always Never

Houndin || Layto

CONCRETE JUNGLE || Bad Omens

Misery || Memphis May Fire

Just Pretend || Bad Omens

Drive You Insane || Angelo Di Angelo

Granite || Sleep Token

don't worry babe || Ex Habit

Lost in Echoes || Caskets

Cross || Echos

Lurk || The Neighbourhood

Talk To a Friend || Rain City Drive

Never Know || Bad Omens

KNIVES || Neoni, Savage Ga$p

Tag, You're It || Melanie Martinez

Beautiful Crime || Tamer

Fire Escape || Call Me Karizma

God Complex || VIOLENT VIRA

You've Created a Monster || Bohnes

Coffin || PLVTINUM

Headache || Asal

High || Stephen Sanchez

Dirty Mind || Boy Epic

Dopamine || Siiickbrain, Maggie Lindemann

Get the full playlist on my website.

https://www.authorrainelyn.com/playlists

AUTHOR'S NOTE

Monstrous Grave is the darkest book I've ever written. It delves into dark and taboo subjects that may be triggering for some readers. If you are uncomfortable with sensitive topics or if any of these warnings may distress you, I strongly urge and beg you to stop reading.

The characters in this book are dark, twisted, and the male character has no morals at all. He's fucked up, unhinged, and will do anything for his own selfish gains, and because he's obsessed. He'll chase you through the woods, stalk you, and then kidnap you, just because "you're his."

The characters in this story are foster siblings, not biologically related, but the narrative explores forbidden themes within the taboo subject as they are raised together.

Monstrous Grave contains explicit sexual content intended for mature readers aged 18 and above. It includes graphic violence, gore, murder, torture, kidnapping, stalking, suicidal ideation, mentions of attempted suicide, destructive behaviors, traumatic events, toxic and possessive behavior, drugging, and fear-inducing scenarios.

Additionally, the book explores various kinks, including somnophilia, consensual non-consent, dubious consent, breath play, blood play, knife play, gun play, primal play, cage, and claustrophobia play (yes, he locks her inside a cage — romantic, right?), praise and degradation, brother-sister kink.

Please proceed with caution.

Your mental health matters.

— Rainelyn xx

A pawn in their lethal game, I became.

A chess player moved around the checkered board with no goal in sight. A withered rose with only thorns left, merely there for entertainment; to keep the enemies' eyes on me. Luring them into the depths of darkness before silently leaving, never once receiving credit for my hard work.

In the shadows, I thrived, a lonely yet compatible space for someone like me. Abandoned, full of sharp thorns that won't yield, discouraging anyone from coming near.

The glowing sun never once touched the corners where I was forced to hide, never once breaking free from the obscurity.

And in those clandestine alleys, I became the enigmatic figure they would come to fear.

The elusive phantom they never anticipated.

They just didn't know it yet.

Without him, I slowly withered away — like a fragile, dead rose trapped within time, never growing or blooming. Internally stagnant, I crumbled day by day, struggling to stay above the surface.

Until one day, everything fell silent.

No more screams inside my head.

No more men taking advantage of me.

A pawn in their lethal game, I perished.

Prologue
Arcane
21 years old

THE NIGHT SKY LOOMS ominously overhead, shrouded in darkness and devoid of stars—a foreboding shadow cast over this sinister mansion.

I wonder if he has sensed it—the tug-of-war between the realms of good and evil, balancing on that line between right and wrong, knowing that one misstep could plunge him into a horror so profound, it threatens to corrupt him.

It's there, isn't it? That festering darkness staining his soul, tearing away at its flesh piece by piece. It's why he seeks solace in my darkness. We're two halves of a cracked mirror, bound by the agony of our shared existence. He slices into my skin with every glance, only to leave me bleeding in his aftermath.

Another sound shatters the stillness, and I snap to attention, the peaceful rhythm of my heart transforming into a wild cadence against the cage of my ribs—almost as if I can feel it beating outside my chest. With fists closing around the duvet, I wait, terror thrumming through my veins. My gaze fixates on the balcony perched on the second floor of this sprawling mansion.

Is it an intruder? If it is, the guards patrolling the perimeters would take care of it. But my foster parents have never cared, especially not my father.

Tonight, even the moon's light fails to calm me, knowing that someone dangerous is waiting outside those doors. Like a warning alarm, every nerve ending in my body buzzes with apprehension.

I glimpse a shadowed figure standing motionless, a silent sentinel with a menacing aura. With wide-open eyes, I stare at him, afraid that if I blink, I'll miss his actions. A force thrashes against the confines of my ribcage, desperate to break free, while I anticipate his strike.

I know it's him; he's always entering my room uninvited.

Yet his presence offers a sense of protection, knowing I'm secure in a world filled with predators. Even with how much I want to deny it, he makes me feel safe in a way no one else can, though we're both corrupted. It's sick, wrong, twisted—are siblings supposed to act like this?

Is it wrong to seek solace in each other after fourteen years of living under the same roof, even if he's only my foster brother?

The shadowy presence observes me, his gaze piercing through

the sheets surrounding my resting frame, and I instinctively pull the duvet tighter around me.

A silent presence in the night, he stands there, merely waiting, watching, observing.

He's lingering outside, not only protecting me but also anticipating the moment when terror will strike me. Then, he will pounce without hesitation.

He wasn't always like this—he used to be kind, with a smile that could shatter your heart with the beauty of it, like a rainbow splitting the sky. Now, his demeanor has grown colder, marked by broken bones and bruises. His once warm manners have been replaced by a chilling one, giving way to an unwavering intensity. He's dangerous. Our father changed him with the family's shady business—dealings I'm not privy to. But, in the dead of the night is where he thrives, and that's when he can truly be himself.

He craves the fear he instills in me. His predatory smirk makes beastly insects fly around my stomach, highlighting the crush I can't have on my fucking brother. I wish there were some way to cut the emotions out, bleeding me dry so I wouldn't feel safe with this predator.

"We're going to play a little game, you and I," he had whispered earlier in the morning, his words laced with mystery.

He refused to elaborate more and left me both intrigued and hesitant, never knowing the true extent of his intentions.

Ever since we met at the orphanage when I was seven and he was nine, there has been an enigmatic force around him that slithered its way into my soul, gripping my heart and refusing to let go.

Our foster parents, who adopted us two years later, remain oblivious to the intricate threads that bind us together. They will never understand the connection we share, nor the despair of being homeless with no one to care for you or keep you safe. They simply see us as two children they took in, expecting our close bond to be severed now that we're adults.

My brother's warnings about our foster parents rang true the moment we first stepped foot into the manor and I saw everyone discreetly wearing guns for the first time. I instantly knew something was off. Our new father's eyes glinted with malice, his jaw ticking with unrelenting anger. Within a month of our arrival, my brother's demeanor shifted, and he became more lethal and aggressive—the hidden traits of his personality filtering through the façade he constructed around me. Other times, he accompanied our father to the shooting range. I never understood the reason for it until years later.

They had shattered his innocence, replacing it with something far more lethal. Days would pass, and I'd catch glimpses of bruises littering his skin, serving as haunting reminders of how much my life had changed since living at the orphanage. We were thrust into a treacherous world, forced to navigate a place where enemies lurked in every corner we hid.

Now, as the years have unfolded, the opulent manor we inhabit is secured by a plethora of guards scattered across the perimeters of our lawn. I find myself sheltered, like a pawn in a game much bigger than I will ever be able to comprehend. All the while, my brother is condemned to endure all the horrors that come with living here.

My eyes land on the figure outside once more, his head tipped back, bathing half of his face in the glowing moonlight. His sharp cheekbones emerge, tracing a confident path against his face—a magnificent masculine elegance.

He observes me the same way I've observed him for the past few weeks, with a sense of foreboding hanging thick in the atmosphere, an intensity that could slice through the air like a knife, and a lethal curiosity.

He watches me with those deep brown eyes that see through the depths of my soul, able to tell my own emotions even when I cannot decipher them myself.

After what feels like an eternity, the balcony door eventually creaks open. The sound echoes within my mind, my heart a madman inside my chest. I can't breathe; the anticipation of what's going to happen wreaks havoc inside of me.

As the door opens all the way, he slips through the opening and steps into my room without making a sound.

Like a dangerous shadow, he pauses on the threshold with a reluctance that makes his shoulders tense. He knows this is wrong—entering my room at night when everyone is none the wiser.

None of that deters my brother, though, as he takes another

step, the balcony door left open behind him. It allows the wind to graze its chilling touch over my bare arms, freezing me underneath the blanket. My breath hitches as he comes forward.

Closer.

Even closer.

Until he stands right by the side of the bed, his brown eyes filled with so much intensity and depth as he takes in my appearance, curling my short hair between his fingertips. It's as if the darkness of the room obscures the color, making them look all black. One eye is swollen, yet another bruise forming that has me swallowing a lump in my throat, especially as it colors him purple and black.

It's a strange combination of hues, and I despise seeing him hurt, nausea churning inside me.

I observe his chest rising and falling, compelled to reach out and touch his cheek, an irresistible urge to draw closer to him. Worry glazes over me as I notice his slight wince before my hand even makes contact. He's quicker than me, capturing my wrist in his large palm and holding it in a tight grip.

The firm shake of his head causes his hair to fall over his eyes, and a look of warning crosses his face.

"Don't touch me," he mouths.

I inhale sharply, tension building in my throat as I fixate on his eyes, nearly covered by long, black lashes that used to make me jealous while growing up. All the girls in school were prettier than me, though my brother always told me I was the prettiest.

He never looked at them the way he looked at me, with equal amounts of adoration and a need to protect.

We were each other's, and no one else had the chance to even get close to us.

Now, all I wish is for him to let me touch him because I can tell that something is wrong, and not only is it the bruise forming on his eye. There's an urgency in his voice, one that jolts through my body in an electric current and causes goosebumps to skitter across my skin.

I allow my gaze to shift to where his hand grips my wrist, still as tightly as before, and then I meet his eyes again, evidently darkening with intensity.

"A game, remember?" he whispers, his voice piercing through the silence that has descended over the room.

An odd sensation overtakes me, like a vise gripping my heart in its hold before squeezing the life out of me. Confusion laces my actions and makes me unable to utter a word. I merely stare at him while he waits for my reply.

I know he's always loved hearing me talk, wanting me to read him bedtime stories even when he's the older one, but now I won't give him the satisfaction of it. He doesn't deserve to hear the sound of my voice when he won't elaborate on what's going on.

It feels like minutes pass when the only thing occupying the room is an intense and uncomfortable silence full of emotions I cannot put into words.

The grip on my wrist hardens, and I do my best not to let out a yelp from the slight burn of pain. That would only make him even more satisfied. Eventually, I'm forced to obey him when the grip never relents, his nails only digging deeper into my skin.

"What kind of game?"

With defiance, I stare into his eyes, although I don't feel nearly as daring as I try to sound. My voice is a hoarse whisper after a night of sleeping, and I'm not as composed as he is.

His demeanor is always posed with a lethal calm that could make the strongest enemy relent, a trait I'm sure he acquired once we were adopted into the Grimaldi family.

The corners of his thick lips twitch into a cryptic smile that gives way for nothing else. "A game of survival."

My eyebrows must be scrunching in confusion because his lips curl further. He stares down at me with a look that has me shuddering, not knowing if I should be afraid or feel safe in his presence.

"You will see, devangel. But it's a game that requires you to be observant. Trust no one but yourself and always keep an eye on your surroundings." His voice is low and demanding, making chills dance across my body while I listen intently, clinging to every word he utters. Especially the nickname he has given me. "Don't crash into the waves."

His last sentence rings out in my head like an echo, words I've heard many times before when I've needed reassurance from the cruel world we live in.

"Trust no one but you, right?"

An audible sigh slips from his lips as he looks down at me, and I observe the subtle tightening of his jaw, a habitual gesture he often displays.

His head tilts to the side, but I cannot tell what it's for. Every action he makes stirs confusion within me, creating a vortex of uncertainty and leaving me slightly rattled. A creeping sense of terror slowly comes into my subconscious, telling me that something might be amiss yet again.

"Can you do that for me?" His serious words take me aback, but despite that, I nod, still unsure of what his intentions are, as my mind races with apprehension.

He has always been a mystery, a puzzle to be solved where I was the only one who had the key to open up the puzzle pieces. Yet, at this moment, it's as if I've lost that key temporarily, unable to understand him.

"Your words, please."

It's the first time I've heard him ask for something.

The sense of urgency emanating from him sparks a desperate impulse in me, an overwhelming desire to claw at his hand and keep him close to me forever. As if I could anchor him to my side by sheer force.

Somewhere deep within my subconscious is a voice telling me this is it.

This is goodbye.

And that makes me want to scream my throat out until there is nothing left within me to fight for.

This is all too cryptic. My throat is clogged with untold emotions that feel like a tumultuous sea, and I am a boat fighting to stay afloat against the lethal waves of death.

I swallow. "Yes."

Nodding his head, he accepts my words for what they are while his fists clench. "Close your eyes." His request is barely a whisper, yet it commands compliance, and I obey.

With my eyes closed tightly shut, my heart pounds hard within me, each thud mirroring the seconds that slowly pass. With a pulse spiking into unnatural heights, it's as if I'm going to pass out at any moment from the anticipation alone. The unmistakable scent of his sandalwood cologne, along with leather—coming from the glove he uses to cover his scarred hand—permeates my nostrils.

My nerves taking over, I glance at the clock standing on my nightstand beside him, noticing that it's 11:59 p.m.

In my periphery, I sense him drawing nearer, and my breath quickens at his closeness. The clock ticks, signaling the start of a new day—midnight.

"Happy birthday, Arcane," he whispers in a hoarse voice that sends butterflies slicing up my insides.

It's a strange concoction of emotions, one entirely unwelcome, with dread seeping through to my marrow and the other inciting a flutter of something visceral within me, akin to a teenage crush.

Without a second to comprehend what's happening, the warmth of his minty breath brushes against my lips. My heart combusts when he presses his lips against mine, punishing in its hold. It's intimate, stirring a storm deep within me.

I allow myself to get lost in the kiss as his tongue prods the seam of my lips, pushing inside, tangling with my own. He's brutal in his kiss, demanding and pushing, never leaving me time to breathe. One hand slides to my throat, encircling it with a pressure that tightens with each passing second, silently demanding my submission. He restricts the air entering my lungs, and a whimper escapes me.

It's a bruising kiss made of lies and deceit.

My eyes close automatically, wanting to savor the feel of his lips on mine. Then, he slips away, his hand leaving my throat and lips leaving mine, and I don't open my eyes. Even long after I hear the balcony door closing and his fragrance subtly fading away from my room, I cannot bring myself to reopen them.

For a short moment after, I find myself smiling, until his strange composure comes back to me, and the weight of that small kiss sends a jolt of despair through my entire being, akin to what I imagine being infected with a flawed vaccine feels like.

It was a wordless and bittersweet farewell etched with tenderness and cruelty as he took my heart in his hold, along with my soul, shredding it apart with his bare hands.

And as dawn breaks, the painful truth hits hard like an unrelenting storm, mercilessly tearing through my fragile peace of mind. The word "dead" lingers in the air, heavy and suffocating coming from my foster parents' mouths.

A train wreck.

He steered me away from an impending crash against the cliffs and the tempting waves that whispered promises of a tranquil descent. In doing so, he spared me from the suffocating yet alluring embrace that could have plunged everything into a serene silence. Ironically, he never followed his own path of advice.

Now, he is gone.

CHAPTER 1
Arcane

26 years old
Present Day

RELENTLESS WAVES BATTER THE steadfast cliffs, wearing away their surface and briefly drowning them in splatters of rain. Their rhythm reflects the chaos within my mind—a state I've been trapped in for years, never finding solace in the twisted world that plagues my being.

Like an unstitched wound, my heart is bleeding out without anything preventing it from withering away. Soon, it will stop beating completely.

I never thought I would come this far, nor did I think it'd be like wading through waves, preparing to submerge until I'm drowned underneath their strong force.

The wind's breeze grabs my hair, messing it up in tangles,

but I remain uncaring. There's not much I care about these days; instead, burning hatred tinged with sorrows takes place, transforming into a poisonous concoction within me.

Hatred—an all too known emotion, potent enough to release toxins throughout you, and with each passing day, the decay intensifies only to spread like a disease until nothing remains.

There was once upon a time when things were good. Better than good—I was happy. Until that happiness shattered like a delicate yet fragile rose amidst sharp thorns, all because of one person who left me.

My attention is captured by the ceaseless assault of waves hurling themselves against the cliffside, resonating with a thunderous roar throughout the caverns below. Tendrils of water climb the rugged walls, eventually spraying over me. I welcome the ocean's embrace, submitting myself to nature's will while wishing the water could sweep me away.

I can't leave yet. Not until I've completed the sole mission I have dedicated my life to for the past five years.

The paper in my hands becomes all the more crinkled as I grip it with such force, it's a wonder it hasn't yet been shredded to pieces. My nails dig into the material, tearing it apart, but it remains readable.

A cold wind steals the warmth from my fingers, removing their flexibility and numbing the tips until I can't feel anything at all.

An unidentifiable droplet falls onto the paper, smudging the inked words. I look up at the darkened sky rumbling with gray clouds, not one ounce of sunlight among them. This time of the year is always bleak, with nothing but rain or overcast, despite it being summer. There's no rain in sight, only the languid clouds hanging motionless in the sky like shadows.

Bringing my hand up to my cheek, something wet touches my skin, and I realize I'm crying. Stupid, pathetic tears over someone who doesn't deserve it or my time. A man whose soul has lived within me for five years since he passed, each day becoming a battlefield in itself made of the unspeakable. A fight I'm incapable of winning.

I grind my teeth until the muscles in my jaw strain, wincing at the tension before allowing my gaze to drift over the cliffs, to the ocean below. It's morbidly beautiful here, with the wind-swept grass standing as sentinels.

Memories of all the times I've been here shift through my mind, and I can only imagine how the ocean floor must be covered with the soaked, torn paper from all my anguished words. It's a wonder the ocean hasn't turned white yet from the thousands of letters I must have thrown over this very cliff, allowing them to gracefully fall before plummeting against the surface below.

Five years ago, you gave me a wordless and bittersweet farewell, leaving me alone in a puddle of tears and my heart's shattered pieces that no one would ever be able to glue or stitch together. You steered me away from an impending crash against these cliffs and the temptation to plummet over the edge, precisely like these letters to you do.

You left me to fend for myself in a game much bigger than I would ever be able to comprehend. No regard whatsoever for the first kiss, orgasm, and pleasure you stole from me before you ripped my heart to pieces.

Did you know? Did you fucking know the pain and tumult you would cause me?

Of course, you knew. Otherwise, you'd have never done what you did.

I miss you so much, but most of all, I fucking hate you for what you did and how you allowed me to fall into a pit of despair after bringing me back alive.

Crumbling the paper in my hands, I shred it into multiple satisfying pieces. With all the arm strength I can gather, I throw them over the edge, observing as the wind takes a hold of them and slowly, gently, brings them down below.

Oh, how I wish the papers could fall as hard and steadily as I fell down a dark pit the moment he left, leaving my heart buried inside a monstrous grave that no one could ever unravel. If only the pieces could feel what I've felt, trying to stay afloat and survive when the only person who ever meant something left me.

Grief and rage are unpredictable, and there's no telling when it will truly strike, leaving you plummeting without any way of climbing up.

Casting one last glance up at the sky, a flash illuminates the heavens for a brief second, like an omen. The silence that ensues is hair-raising, the seconds after the flash but before the thunder, and then it strikes, rolling over my surroundings. The first glistening droplets fall from above, instantly chilling me.

At that moment, an anguished scream tears its way free from

my lips, my throat burning and soaring with the rawness of the sound as it echoes between the cliff walls, resonating back and forth until it eventually fades before beginning again.

I scream until there's nothing left inside of me, the excruciating pain gradually subsiding and leaving a scar right across my soul. The roar of sorrow persists until I'm on the verge of breathlessness, the anguish diminishing for now, until the moment I have to drive to the cliffs once more and repeat the same process.

This is the only refuge that silences the tumultuous voices in my head, muting the darkness that might otherwise lead me to kill anyone who dares come close.

He ruined me in the worst ways any human could ruin someone, destroying me from the inside out when he left me. When he died, the only living piece remaining inside me was killed with his essence. Now? I'm just an empty shell of a person trying to navigate through an underground world of horrors and crimes that I shouldn't even be a part of.

I turn my back to the sea, silently longing for a phantom push to nudge me off balance, sending me slipping over the edge into the peace my soul has yearned for. Instead, I head toward my motorbike parked by the dirt road, straightening my spine to regain some composure.

It's never enough, but that doesn't matter because vengeance is close. Anticipation thrums through my veins like a buzzing current as I think back to it all.

Justice will be served to all those who wronged me. If only I could resurrect him, just to make him witness the hatred etched deep into my soul the moment before I'd wrench his neck free from his body.

If only.

Chapter 2
Arcane

AS I ENTER THE pristine white marble, its opulent estate boasting a beautifully tended garden behind me, the halls are eerily quiet. Drenched from the relentless rain that intensified the faster I pushed my bike forward, I remove my sodden leather jacket upon stepping inside, revealing the tattoo on my arm. It's a butterfly surrounded by water, reminiscent of how I felt when *he* left, yet a reminder that I can and will survive.

The grandeur of the hall, adorned with a hanging chandelier and crystal decorations, greets me as I navigate the three-building mansion. A swirl of discomfort twists in my stomach, leaving me with a parched mouth. The absence of the usual activity— no bustling kitchen staff or guards—only intensifies my apprehension.

With a frown, I hear faint murmurs from the room ahead. Something is amiss; I feel it in the way goosebumps skitter across my arms.

"Arcane, is that you?" A deep voice cuts through the silence, drawing me closer to the conference room.

I swallow hard, knowing all too well that there is no possibility of escaping this life I've found myself trapped in. It isn't as if I can leave—they won't let me get away. I owe them my life after they saved mine.

Soon, a man stands before me, dressed in a well-tailored suit with his tie hanging loose and hair tousled in disarray. His gaze, reminiscent of his father's, sweeps over me, making me squirm. He has gotten his father's eyes, that's for sure. Large and piercing, beautiful yet holding a lethal glint.

"Hi, Alec."

He cocks his head to the side, an uneasy expression flickering across his face—a subtle indication that there's something he's not telling me, something he knows that I don't. Something I won't like.

I eye the opening of the conference room, nervous energy coursing through me. The room is rather large, adorned with a whiteboard at the front displaying a meticulously planned heist, including photos of all the targets and red dots on a map. At the forefront stands our boss, his presence emanating a shrouded force, veiled in darkness and lethality. Standing beside him is his right-hand man, Antonio Cadell, while positioned at the room's rear are our most trusted made men—ranked lowest, commanding respect nonetheless. They have all sworn an oath of silence and committed deceitful acts to secure their place within our organization.

Alec closes the door behind us, and I suppress the rapid pounding of my heart with an almost bored expression. I cannot show any sign of hesitation.

I feel our boss's piercing eyes dissecting me with an intensity that drags up memories I would rather forget. They take me back to a past life, a girl I once was who isn't me anymore, now forever lost. The weight of his gaze transports me to the unforgiving streets, where I had to survive on my own without having anything to myself. I remember his gaze back then, bothering and terrifying me, until Alec dared show a glimmer of humanity. He took my dirty hand in his, offering me a smile as he helped me to my feet, dirt and mud clinging to every inch of my skin.

Benjamin Valenti looks at me in the same way he did five years ago the moment he found me, seeing the youthful rage and hatred in me. He's not someone you'd want to fuck over.

He exudes fear and respect, demanding the latter by instilling terror in those around him. Even the slightest transgression, like someone cheating in his illegal casinos, is met by brutality. A single dollar stolen can lead to blood splattered all over the room in a sight too grotesque for most to accept, with screams reverberating through the room. A single misplaced word is enough for entrails to be exposed and the echoes of a once-functioning brain to be cleaved apart.

I was both lucky and not that they found me, forcing me into this shadowed world of criminality and secrecy. Once you're in, there's no way out unless it's in a body bag. I'm ensnared here, trapped against my own will, and have been for the past five years since my parents kicked me out on the streets.

The criminal life is not for me. *He* is the reason my innocence was killed long before I could truly explore who I was, all my dreams drowned in the waves, only to never return.

He left me when all I needed was him by my side, us against the world when nothing else mattered.

He fucking ruined me.

And now, I'm thrust into this world with nowhere to go, a rage burning inside my veins that I cannot release. There's a snake within me, slithering in my blood, crawling through me with the toxin of rage that makes it impossible to control my own emotions some days.

I stare at Mr. Valenti leaning casually against the desk, his well-maintained physique belying his age. A smirk hints at his lips, one full of resilience.

I fucking hate him too, but at least he's preferable to the parents who abandoned me. At least he took me in when no one else would, even though it came with its own set of consequences.

Benjamin possesses an uncanny ability to manipulate me, exploiting my desire for revenge and promising me all the things I've ever wanted. This is what keeps me leashed to his side.

Alec is like the best friend I lost all those years ago, slowly stitching together my broken heart and the pieces *he* tore out. In a world where trust is a scarce commodity, his loyalty has been unwavering; always watching out for me, caring about me, and understanding the need for revenge I've sought for so long.

"What took you so long?" a voice barks at me, and I try to suppress my evident annoyance as I turn to look at Mr. Valenti.

"If I had known earlier, I would have arrived much sooner," I mutter irritably.

Mr. Valenti shoots a glance at his son, the tension in the room palpable.

"Sit," Mr. Valenti demands, and I feel my heart beating hard inside my chest as I settle down in one of the chairs while intently listening.

Blood rushes in my ears like a relentless force with the knowledge that I'm one step closer to proving my fucking worth in this world where no one believes in me.

For far too long, I became a pawn in their games, a woman they could do whatever they wanted with. I've always been a chess player who was moved around the board without any particular goal except to entertain the men around me or keep the eyes of the enemies locked on me, luring them into the depths of the darkness.

I've always known I had bigger dreams than becoming a toy for men who have no regard for others, and executing this heist will be the final nail in the coffin, sealing my fate and proving my worth.

Alec locks eyes with me, seemingly able to decipher my thoughts. His encouraging smile draws one from me in return.

The only other person who treated me the way a woman should be treated except for Alec, was *him*. His name is forbidden to speak aloud. Like a ball of firecrackers, he entered my world when we were mere children, crashing and colliding with my universe until there was nothing left but the two of us. He made me feel things no one ever had. His gaze on me whispered things that made the butterflies in my stomach stutter and fly around in a chaotic whirlwind, and though he was so young and innocent, I knew he was the darker half of my soul.

The one I never wanted to be separated from.

Thinking about all the misdeeds we committed at the orphanage makes an unknown smile twitch my lips. Such a foreign emotion, I'm barely even aware of what the sensation within me is.

I quickly conceal the smile when the reality comes washing over me, a dreaded whisper lingering inside my mind, haunting and threatening me. His words. Cold, calculated words that cut through me like the sharpest knife.

"We're going to play a game, you and I."

It fucking hurts to think about the past and all he did to break my heart when he left. I fucking hate him for it. I fight my hardest to concentrate on what Mr. Valenti is about to say, his gaze sweeping over both Alec and me.

"Things are worse than we predicted. It means a power game is at play, with us and the entire town as the chessboard about to meet a brutal death, like peasants taken to slaughter."

My leg bounces up and down as he continues his speech, the truth hitting me in my stomach like the hardest punch, as if it's stealing my very breath.

"We know the real intel we seek holds the power capable of disrupting the underground's order. We need to get that information immediately—secure the car and obliterate everything inside, unless we all want to fucking face defeat."

His eyes meet mine once more, a lethal force that tempts me to avert my gaze, yet I hold it, my determination never wavering. I nod, already understanding the importance of this heist.

We must secure the car before the Grimaldi family seizes it. Inside lies highly sensitive information, that if uncovered, could doom us all. It contains details about all the families' criminal activities, connections, and alliances that the Valentis have gathered throughout the years, information that allows them to gain power and leverage within the criminal world. But now, the USB drive has been stolen and sold inside a car on the black market, offering the traitor a fortune. The Grimaldis, unaware of its contents, saw it as a valuable asset. Once they acquire it, they might decrypt its content, putting every organization at risk if the sensitive information were to be leaked.

The thief is a rat, pretending to be one of our associates, working his way up in the hierarchy of our world, well on his way to truly joining us as a so-called made man.

That motherfucker cunningly stole it under a gala event he wasn't even supposed to attend, which is how we ended up in this situation to even begin with.

I'd like to think I haven't always been a violent person, seeking the pain of others, watching the blood gush from broken noses or torn flesh wounds.

I wasn't always like this. These emotions within me have become bottled up, only fueled by the betrayal of the Grimaldis. I want to spit on their graves and break their gravestones until the surrounding relatives crave the answers as to who would dare do such heinous acts. And if these relatives discover it was me, I'll kill them too. I'll spill the blood of the family that failed me when all I craved was their fucking love and care, when my soul withered away inside.

Too bad they aren't in their graves.

Not yet, at least.

Retribution and revenge are close. I can practically feel the sweet taste on my tongue.

The look in Mr. Valenti's eyes, hardened and unmoving—not even flickering or blinking—tells me that what he's about to say next will change it all. Even his straightened posture screams determination, every muscle in his body molded into a stance of unyielding resolve. I wait with bated breath to hear his next words.

"I made my decision a long time ago. You will have a companion with you during this heist."

His words have my mouth gaping open before I quickly close it, my nails pressing so hard into my palms that I feel the skin breaking underneath the forceful dig.

It's as if my lungs refuse to draw in a breath of air when I look at him.

"Who?" I don't mean to sound so fucking pathetic or breathy when asking about the person, yet his statement caught me completely off guard.

This wasn't what we agreed upon. What. The. Fuck?

I cast a side glance at Alec, his expression as indifferent as his father's, seeing if he knew anything about this. Surely, Mr. Valenti must mean that I'll be working with Alec?

Settling down at the head of the table standing in the center of his office, Mr. Valenti runs a hand through his hair before his eyes meet mine once again. He notices me looking at Alec and shakes his head.

"No, not my son. You're going to work with Viper on this one."

He drops the bomb with no regard whatsoever to me, his eyes penetrating through my soul while giving me that cold, calculating look as he waits for his words to hit me like an explosion. My face drains of all color, leaving behind a ghostly pallor. It's as if a cold breeze from outside has slithered inside, sweeping through the room and stealing the very warmth that keeps me alive. Another second passes while a white-hot, blaring rage runs through my veins, poisoning me.

"Viper?" The words involuntarily slip out before I have the

chance to stop them from tumbling out.

Viper, the notorious masked biker who's involved in the worst criminal underground family this country has. He's well-known in our world, rivaling with the Valenti family—much like all other organizations in this city. Yet, the fact that the name *Viper* just slipped out from Mr. Valenti's lips stuns me the fuck out, having seen his hatred for the cartel Viper is involved in for years. Why in the world would they want to work with him?

He's ruthless, uses cunning tactics, and has an unrelenting appetite for chaos in our world. As the rumors go, he's the second-born son to the García cartel, but when a tragic accident happened way before I moved into the Valenti house, the second-born was forced to step up. He's assumed to take over the García cartel once his old man steps down, but I have no idea how that shit will go. The man is a lone wolf through and through. Yet, much like the cartel's reputation, his presence is known before one even crosses his path. Rarely seen in public, he exists as both a ghost and a tangible threat—someone who methodically devours his prey, opting for gradual consumption rather than a quick and painless disassembling. He is more lethal than a katana sword cutting straight through you.

At this point, I can almost feel the blood rushing through my body like a pot of water left on the stove for too long. Mr. Valenti stares at me with equal parts annoyance and satisfaction, with a twitch of his lips. I wouldn't have noticed it had I not stared right at his face—disrespecting him further—but the shock is too evident in my expression.

Alec isn't nearly as tense as I am; instead his posture is relaxed and composed, as if he isn't even bothered by this revelation. The fucker knew about this, and he told me nothing.

"What the fuck for?" I growl, unable to stop the reaction from coming out of my mouth once again.

Oh God, I'm in so much trouble.

Mr. Valenti's steely gaze meets mine as an ice-cold feeling washes over me, like a bucket of cold water that's been left out in the Arctic.

"There's no room for disobedience here. Remember your place, *girl*, and who took you in when no one wanted you," he spits out, saliva flying out of his mouth, only landing a few centimeters away from me.

Fucking disgusting.

His words are meant to hurt me, but all they do is further anger me, pouring gasoline on the rage waring within my body.

"Understood," I grit through my teeth.

The prospect of having to work with a bastard fucking biker with no regard for anyone else is akin to dancing on the precipice of danger and unpredictability, especially since this was *my* fucking heist. Unfortunately, my fate is sealed by the words of a man I both despise and owe my allegiance to, making me hate him even more.

Annoyance ripples through me once again, stronger than before, as I stand to leave the room. I hear their voices calling out for me, but I refuse to back down and continue walking.

Fuck them both.

Chapter 3
Arcane
18 years old

"YOU DON'T LAY A finger on her, and you certainly don't fucking look at her. If I catch you doing it one more time, I'll put you down like the pathetic little dog you are."

His words slice through the atmosphere like a knife, each one carrying a threat that echoes in the world around us. The wind carries them, creating an unsettling sound that will surely draw onlookers, forming a circling crowd around us. Kaiden's back is turned to me, his muscles flexing with each deliberate step toward the other boy—Leo, a fucking cowardly boy who still manages to tear down my confidence with words and falsely spread lies. I can't help but bite my lip, watching with hesitation as the scene unfurls before me.

This wasn't how the end of my school day was supposed to turn out, and the bitter taste of bile lingers on the back of my tongue.

"Are we clear?"

The words spewing from my foster brother's mouth are filled with such indifference, you wouldn't know he's threatening someone. His demeanor is cool, calm, and collected, as if this is a normal occurrence for him.

Minutes tick by, the only audible sounds are the footsteps coming closer. Leo's silence hangs heavily in the air as I stand in the middle of the crowd, my face flushed and palms sweaty from the rush of adrenaline pulsing through me. I *hate* violence, despise it, even. Yet there's something in the way Kaiden protects me that makes a fluttering sensation take root deep within my stomach, creeping closer to my most sensitive part.

Throughout the years, my attraction for my foster brother has only intensified, making it impossible to be in the same room as him without my heart pounding and my body on edge. *Goddamn hormones.* At this point, I'm certain Kaiden has noticed my feelings, judging by his deliberate teasing—like showing up in my room wearing nothing but a towel or invading my personal space with that smirk of his. He's infuriating, especially when he sneaks through my window at night, tucking me into bed, pressing his body close to mine. He's always seeking to touch and provoke me, and it drives me mad.

Low whispers come from the crowd, and without a second's

hesitation, Kaiden's fist meets Leo's face, sending him tumbling to the ground. A high-pitched shrill is heard across the schoolyard, drawing the attention of nearby students who begin to approach.

Fuck, this isn't good at all.

I make my way over to my foster brother, gripping his arm while attempting to tug him away. He tears his gaze away from Leo, his lips busted and coated with blood as it slowly dries.

"Let's go," I mumble urgently.

Leo rises, legs unsteady, but his expression betrays emotions I'd rather not confront. "She's a fucking bitch," he sneers.

The lethal darkness taking over my foster brother's eyes is alarming, making unease travel down my spine in violent shivers. Another glint replaces the previous calm façade Kaiden wore on the surface; now he looks as if he's ready to murder Leo with his bare fists.

I swallow what feels like molten lava running down my throat as I attempt to tug at his sleeve again, but it's too late. He gently releases my grip, stalking toward Leo before grabbing him by his collar. Leo starts choking, sputtering out words, but the rage is all too prominent in my brother. There's no restraining him when he's like this; his temperament only worsens by the day.

Kaiden slams Leo down on the cobblestoned ground, his head smashing against it and making a sickening sound.

Another shrill echoes through the yard, people screaming for my brother to stop while others urge him on. The moment I hear the creaking of the doors of the school building, my head whips in that direction, my heart skipping a beat as an urgent alarm rings through my head. I run over to Kaiden, tugging at his arm harder this time.

For a short second, he looks down at me before noticing the principal and other teachers making their way down the staircase, advancing on us.

"Fuck," he curses under his breath, though the glint in his eyes tells me of his mischievous thoughts.

Grabbing my hand in his, he dashes toward his bike, parked just a few meters away as the crowd—still gathered around us—disperses. Rage still swirls in his irises, but some of the tension has been released, and I cannot even muster any sympathy for Leo or the pain caused to him.

Leo's cruel taunts sting like salt in a fresh wound, dredging up memories of my past as an orphan living with foster parents. Despite his incessant jabs, I can't seem to gather enough courage to stand up against him, making my self-loathing only deepen.

But just when things started becoming worse at the schoolyard, my foster brother arrived to pick me up. Riding on his bike has always been an escape for me, a brief respite from the turmoil of real life. Today, it seems like luck is on my side—sort of.

He throws me the helmet, and I hastily secure it in place. Without another minute to spare, Kaiden revs the engine and is out of the parking lot, heading toward the forest.

Then, we drive away, escaping school and leaving the responsibilities behind us.

HIS LAUGHTER ECHOES THROUGH the trees, his smile a beautiful wonder that makes my lips stretch, a sense of safety filling me in this world of bleakness, where nothing seems to matter anymore. I run as fast as my legs can take me away from him while giggling.

This is happiness, I think.

Moments where the sorrow of my abandonment doesn't overwhelm me, when the pain and loneliness don't make me want to give up on life. Depression is an odd feeling, especially when you're feeling fine on certain days, but others are a mere hell to live through. Some days, the world around me continues to taunt me for existing while I'm a mere shell inside my body. Other times, fleeting moments of joy fill me, only to die, leaving me stumbling in the darkness that welcomes me.

I'm good at pretending that everything is fine, when in fact, nothing is. A smile plastered on my lips lets people know I'm okay, even though it's far from the truth.

"I'll get you!" Kaiden shouts, a chuckle erupting from his lips, making a smile split my own.

With him, I'm more myself than I've ever been. My foster brother is the only person who has ever been there for me, loving me when no one else did, and protecting me from people like Leo who hurt me with their words.

So what if our relationship defies what society deems as

normal?

My legs carry me through the casket of trees, determined to keep my emotions at bay. Kaiden will only taunt me if I start crying. According to him, crying reveals vulnerabilities that others could exploit. Besides, I refuse to appear weak before him, especially since he's always been so strong for me.

Twigs rip against my bare arms as I rush past them, not letting them deter me from how fast I move forward. I barely even notice the pain erupting from their claws as I flee from my foster brother.

"Stop running, little sister," he shouts behind me.

One of his favorite games is tag, and now, he's 'it.'

A wave of fear crashes over me, sending shivers down my spine as a rush of panic floods my senses. I'm urged to run faster, escape his reach no matter what.

"One of these days, I'll catch you, little sister." His voice weaves through the trees, a chilling caress tingling my skin. "And when I do, you'll beg me to let you go."

In a moment of carelessness, my body tumbles to the wet grass as my knees scrape against the smattering of gravel. I yelp, tears burning behind my eyes. *Embarrassing.*

Kaiden catches up to me, his lips twitching up into a smirk as he towers over me, a glint of satisfaction in his eyes, blended with a flicker of vulnerability hinting at concern.

"Got you, little sister," he murmurs, his voice huskier, sending shivers down my spine.

My heart pounds like a madman from the way he emphasized

each syllable, his voice deepening, growing darker and more intense. Involuntarily, I find myself clenching my thighs, a sudden surge of heat between the two of us.

"You have to be careful," he says, crouching down before me, suddenly too close for my comfort.

His closeness makes my breath hitch, and I pray he doesn't notice it. I'm gulping as I look at him through glazed eyes, watching the concern fade away from his expression and be replaced by a calculated one.

I remember our first encounter—his eyes connecting with mine in a heart-warming sensation. It was the day he arrived at the orphanage. Unlike me who grew up with no parents at all, Kaiden had his mother until she died when he was nine years old. That was when he was sent to the house where I lived.

Over the years, the warmth in his eyes gradually faded away, replaced by an increasing coldness that the years only hardened. Our foster father made sure to dim the light in him. Despite that, I know he tries to fight against his inner demons, striving to be a better person for my sake.

"Princesses don't cry. In this world we live in, you have to be strong. You're crumbling apart, and it's not a pretty look." His words cut through the air with acute precision.

Anger simmers within me, bubbling like a pot ready to boil over. I frown at him. "Fuck you."

His hand is suddenly on my throat, staring down at me with those cold eyes that could pierce through anything. I feel myself gulping underneath his touch, still trusting him not to hurt me.

I'm twisted.

"That's not a way to treat your brother, princess," he admonishes, tone laced with authority.

Beneath my shirt, my nipples stiffen, and I can't discern if it's the chilly wind rustling through the trees or his nearness that causes this fiery reaction. His gaze feels like a scorching caress against my skin as if his eyes are methodically stripping me down with each passing second. I can't help but notice the hunger in him, though I could be misinterpreting the situation.

I don't reply despite the retort clinging to my tongue and begging to be let out. Instead, I wait for the moment he'll let go of my throat. I'm aware he can feel the quickening thud of my pulse beneath his palm, each beat reverberating through his body as he maintains control over me. The rhythmic *thud, thud, thud* is only a testament to the control he has over me, my pulse beating even harder whenever he is nearby.

"How does it feel? Your life is in my hands," he mumbles under his breath, yet despite his low tone, it's as if he's screaming in my ears. "Like it's always been. If I put enough pressure here…" His words whisper a threat, something that my body can't seem to fully grasp.

My feet remain rooted in place, waiting with bated breath for his next move. His other hand strokes my cheek, trailing toward my neck, and the gaze in his eyes tells me he could very well do what he threatened to do. I should run, get as far away from him as possible. Yet, I don't want to, because despite it all, I know I'm safe with him.

"…Your brain won't receive enough oxygen. I'm the only one allowed to kill you. Understood?" he continues.

His words are cryptic and cold, his last sentence hitting me straight to my heart like a gunshot. He is referring to the fact that my mental health has been declining throughout the years, slowly turning me into a withered rose that's losing her petals day by day. Being forced to see a therapist has not helped. The only person I've been able to fully open up to has been him, like an anchor in a stormy sea keeping me afloat, yet a hellhound.

That's the thing about having rich, uncaring parents. They pay hundreds of dollars for a therapist, brushing issues like mental illness under the rug and pretending they never existed. As long as the therapist is doing their job, the parents can go back on their merry little way.

He squeezes harder, slowly restricting the oxygen from my lungs. Eventually, they start burning slightly, deprived of air.

"Understood?" he growls, and I nod, never once breaking eye contact.

He finally eases his grip on my throat, allowing me to gasp for breath. I'm embarrassingly turned on right now, but I won't ever admit it. His eyes slide down to my thighs, now clenching even tighter, and his eyebrows rise, a smirk hinting at his lips.

I swallow, my throat dry with anticipation, as I see the thick outline of his crotch—a bulge growing more prominent by the second. His hand suddenly lands on my thigh, grabbing it harshly, sending a jolt of electricity through me. I can't help but notice the prominent veins tracing his skin, highlighted by the sunlight filtering through the trees.

Is he…aroused?

Does he feel the same intoxicating sensations as I do?

I shake my head internally, dismissing that thought as soon as it comes to me.

"If you're making demands, so should I," I bite back while dragging in enough oxygen, watching his gaze zeroing in on me. "You could have been arrested for assault back there!" I sound more upset than I intended to be.

Kaiden merely shrugs his shoulders. "But I wasn't." The look in his eyes tells me how satisfied he is with that outcome.

"Arrogant bastard," I mutter under my breath.

With a sudden move, his thumb traces a path along my thigh, sending shivers of anticipation sweeping over me. His touch inches closer to the pulsating heat between my legs while his eyes are still connected to mine. My heart pounds heavily, sweat dampening my palms, as emotions overwhelm me. A wave of hesitation crashes over me while a rational voice in my mind urges caution.

"I… You're my brother," I whisper, attempting to pull away from him, but the slick grass delays my movements.

"So what? I don't care."

Without a word, his hand ventures toward the apex of my thighs, drawing closer to the hem of my shorts. I try to maintain my composure, not wanting him to see how deeply his touch affects me. Biting down on my lip, I suppress the faint moan threatening to escape as his fingers trace the seam of my shorts. A wildfire spreads through me. I can't act or do anything at all when he has me under his spell. He maneuvers me like a puppeteer, keeping me on my toes with strings.

He doesn't utter a word as his hand grazes my core, a burning sensation taking root within me. He applies slight pressure, touching just the right spot as he begins to circle my clit with precision. Despite my efforts to resist, the moan I held back escapes, his skillful touch coaxing it from me. I glimpse the hard cock straining against his jeans, suddenly filled with the urge to touch and taste him. He expertly draws waves of pleasure from me, each touch sending me into ecstasy. I fight to keep myself grounded, not to let the emotions overtake me. Our ragged breaths mingle in the peaceful woods, echoing our carnal yearnings for each other.

Another uncontrollable moan escapes my lips, and I've never felt anything quite like this before. The moments of touching myself at night, using my vibrator on my clit while fingers slipped between my folds at the thought of him, pales in comparison to the reality of his touch. It's as if he has done this before. That thought is sickening, and I instantly remember where we are and who it is that's giving me this feeling of bliss.

With all the remaining shreds of my dignity, I scramble backward, meeting his gaze now full of simmering rage. I clench my legs together, cursing myself for allowing that bliss to be taken away from me—*I was so close.*

His nails dig into my thighs, drawing blood, and I observe his hungry expression as he sees the crimson stains painting my flesh.

"Kaiden, we can't do this," I whisper, my voice quivering with a mix of adrenaline, arousal, and fear.

His eyes darken, the brown orbs shifting with conflicting emotions. "You're my property. You belong to me. I can do whatever I want."

I swallow harshly.

Shaking my head at him, I deny the obvious truth. "You're delusional."

His fingers find my throat once more, squeezing ever so tightly, with seething rage as his breaths become labored. The rage makes me nervous, my nipples pebbling under my shirt. *Something is seriously wrong with me.*

He's about to say something back when his phone suddenly rings, the sound filling the tense atmosphere around us in the clearing of the forest. He lets go of my throat, grabs his phone from the back pocket of his jeans, and answers it.

While he's on the phone, I can't help but steal glances at him, taking in the sight of his well-defined physique filling out his clothes better now that he's grown up. Twenty to my eighteen. His toned muscles flex subtly beneath the fabric, and I shift my gaze to his face.

Bathed in the embrace of the afternoon sun, his hair becomes a mesmerizing cascade of honeyed strands, capturing every ray. The golden hues of his locks shimmer, framing his face with a warmth that seems to melt away the otherwise cold expression on his face.

I can't help but feel the dreaded butterflies flying around in my belly, along with the arousal coating my panties—dangerous and deadly, bleeding me dry from the heartache of having these unknown emotions.

When he finally puts down his phone, his stormy eyes meet mine, and he smirks at me, all traces of his earlier rage gone. "Mom wants us home for dinner to plan your birthday next week. It'll give you the time to hide that flush on your cheeks," he cheekily says, his lips twitching in a wider smirk.

I can't help but blush even more, feeling the frustration of the orgasm I didn't get.

What the fuck is wrong with me?

Chapter 4
Arcane
Present Day

THE ACRID STENCH OF gasoline claws at my senses as I push the bike harder, faster, trying to outrun the memories. My heart pounds with thoughts of yesterday's meeting with the Valentis, a relentless echo throbbing inside my skull.

"You're going to work with Viper García."

The very thought makes me shudder, and bile leaves a sickening taste that refuses to fade. Taking a deep breath of air, I realize it does nothing to help the persistent voice inside my head.

I owe them everything for saving me from the streets, but it doesn't erase the dislike I feel toward Benjamin Valenti.

I feel like I'm losing my mind, driving forward with no goal in sight in a fruitless attempt to clear my head. The harder I try, the more oppressive the thoughts grow. Glancing down at the speedometer, I realize I'm barreling down these narrow asphalt roads with no control.

The tires betray me, losing traction as the bike careens out of control. A deafening screech fills my surroundings, drowning out all other sounds as I'm thrown forward, clinging to the handlebars for dear life. With a desperate twist of my wrists, I press down the brakes, the bike skidding to a halt with a final, earsplitting screech. Adrenaline paralyzes my body, my hands trembling as I pry them from the handlebars. Sweat beads on my forehead, mingled with the sheer fright that filled my veins only moments ago.

What the fuck just happened?

I've never lost control like that before.

I'm shaking from the shock as I decide it's best to clear my thoughts now when I'm not riding with the wind. Turning off the engine on my black Kawasaki, I remove my helmet and sit down on the grassy patch beside the slight slope. Next to the road lies a field that stretches out before meeting a dense forest—a familiar sight, one I've passed by many times.

As the wind tousles the shorter strands of my platinum hair, I draw my knees up to my chest, leaning back on my hands. Before me, the horizon unfolds, stretching out endlessly.

When did my life become so messed up? Full of betrayal, deceit, lies.

I take the gun from my holster, its weight familiar and comforting in my hand. I'm supposed to meet up with that biker now to carry out Alec's plan, although here I am. The main part is to steal shipments meant for delivery to the Grimaldi syndicate in three weeks. These people are heavily involved in loansharking, and intel from underground sources in the black market has let us know they've acquired a car shipment through their predatory deals. Unfortunately, the rat who betrayed us got hold of this important shipment and successfully sold it on the market. Now, it's on its way to getting into even worse hands.

I've already promised myself that I'll be doing this myself. It's my revenge against the Grimaldis, who cast me out when they deemed me unworthy of being their child. Little does Mr. Valenti know that I'm too goddamn stubborn. I don't ever do something I don't want to. It's not like I believe he's going to figure it out, but I still haven't grasped why he wants me to work with Viper García.

With a groan, I close my eyes, waiting for my head to stop spinning and my thoughts to clear.

Just the distraction I need—a sudden sound breaks my thoughts, and I swiftly look back, heart thrumming wildly.

No one is there.

I keep looking around, searching for anything amiss, but the only things noticeable are two deer farther off in the fields, with the sun gradually dipping below the horizon. Sweat coats my palms when I catch sight of something far away on the abandoned road—closer to the forest than I am, yet too close for my comfort.

A bike.

A biker.

My heart beats erratically when the low hum of the engine turns off. The organ in my chest resembles a frantic deer, skittering inside me as it runs in panic from the sound of the engine. The feeling of dread spreads through me like a relentless wave, not giving way for mercy as I stare at the biker.

Despite how far off he is, I notice his wider shoulders, taller frame, hinting that it's a man standing there. I swallow harshly, holding as still as I can, never daring to move or even breathe.

Be still, and he won't see you.

Of course he will fucking see me. We're in the middle of nowhere.

The figure stands motionless, helmet covering his face, shoulders clad in a black leather jacket and hands in leather gloves. He's protected from head to toe in leather, his frame never wavering from the seat of his bike. I don't know what to do, panic clawing at me from the inside.

Think, think, fucking think!

The thought of calling Alec for backup crosses my mind, but then, I'm not in the mood to speak to him. Not after yesterday, or after realizing he knew I had to work with someone else without informing me or intervening. Especially not since I'm supposed to be at the dock right now.

There's something in the way the stranger observes me that I can sense even from afar. Though I cannot see his eyes, I feel his gaze on me.

I don't know what to do or how to react, sitting utterly still as he observes me. Soon, the sun will disappear entirely, leaving me alone with this stranger on the abandoned road. With a shaky breath, I grip the gun even tighter, never breaking my gaze from the masked stranger.

When he doesn't move, I decide to take a chance and rise to my feet, slowly stepping over to my bike. I draw in a breath when I see his hand twitching, the low hum of his Yamaha R1 starting. It gleams under the remnants of daylight, curving with precision and painted in a mesmerizing combination of black and red.

I start mine, attempting to maintain my composure. He zeroes in on me, sending a churn of anxiety deep within me. I secure my helmet and start to drive away from the side of the road where I parked.

He does the same.

Think!

Could it be him? The notorious biker? I've never seen him in real life, but he's all over news articles.

I swallow the lump of saliva that sticks like glue in my throat, a bitter taste filling me when I rev the engine.

Once more, he does the same. *What the hell?*

Without hesitation, I grab the gun and point it backward, firing with as much accuracy as I can muster without even looking. It doesn't seem to deter him, and I fire another shot, praying it'll hit my target. I don't care if I end up killing him—I just need him off my tail.

The screech of wheels behind me lets me know I must have

punctured his tire. Seizing the moment of distraction, I push the bike at an even faster speed, leaving the stranger behind on the abandoned road, with my pulse pounding like a drumbeat in my frantic need to escape.

Chapter 5
Arcane

SOME DAYS ARE WORSE than others. On those occasions, my chest feels as if it's ripped apart by pain, a seed taking root within, only to never let go. Before him, solitude was my constant companion, with no friends to speak to back at the orphanage. I understood them because why would anyone befriend the quiet, weird girl who barely dared speak to someone?

Then, *he* intruded upon my world when I was seven years old. Through teasing and taunting, he eventually made me snap, and I spoke for the first time in years. His response was nothing but a grin, a captivating, calculated smirk playing upon his lips.

That was the day I realized he was something else, a boy unlike anyone I had ever met before, with a dark sense of humor no one but I could understand.

"We are meant to be together. You're mine."

His words were possessive. His actions told me I was to be his, and I yearned for a big brother to look up to, someone who would care about me in ways no one else ever had.

Now, I find myself alone in a world he vowed to stay in. A liar, a manipulator, a goddamn thief who stole my trust and heart.

My fingers dance across the keyboard as I infiltrate the Grimaldis' security system with ease, effortlessly deactivating their alarms for thirty minutes. I have Mr. Valenti's right-hand man to thank for my proficiency in hacking. I know it wasn't in my best interest at heart; they did it for their own selfish reasons, like every other syndicate in this twisted town, where the underbelly controls it all.

I never showed up at the meeting yesterday, and something tells me neither did Viper. According to Mr. Valenti and Alec, we're supposed to meet again today, but I disregarded their demand and went straight to the dock instead. I've already gathered all the necessary information from the outside, taking photos of the dock and the Grimaldis' submarine stationed nearby, and now I'm working to deactivate their alarms so I can get a better look inside. This is the largest dock in Penumbra Crest, situated on the other side of town where buildings are sparse and civilization is scarce. I don't understand why I have to work with another person for this mission. It's so goddamn easy alone, especially as no guards work here on Sundays.

I know what dire consequences might befall me when Mr. Valenti finds out I ghosted Viper. But he and his misogyny can go fuck themselves with a stick up their asses. If this heist is going to go as smoothly as possible, it's better if fewer people know about it.

We can't have the other organizations finding out about this, especially not the Grimaldis. I certainly do not trust the Garcías enough to let them in on this shit. I'm a loner and observer, having survived by myself for so long that I cannot depend on others anymore.

The screen illuminates the shed they use as a guard station, providing shelter as I work on installing a driver into their security system. When the light turns green, indicating the successful deactivation, I instantly remove the drive from their computer. I secure the ski mask over my head, tucking my short hair into it, and adjust my leather jacket before slipping out into the darkness. Cautiously, I make my way toward the looming main building, the night shrouded by an unsettling fog.

The wind is a haunting whistle in the distance as I stride toward the front of the building I spotted while taking the photos I sent over to Alec. The faint scent of salty water fills my nostrils, and the boards of the dock creak underneath my weight as I approach the bridge leading to the building. There's no one nearby, yet I quicken my pace, determined to complete this part of the mission and leave as soon as possible.

Drawing closer, I observe its sturdy brick construction, with its small windows barred, offering no glimpses of the activity hidden within. I stick to the walls as I sneak closer, eventually reaching the main door. With a deep breath—fearing the alarms might still be active—I open the door, one hand on my gun, prepared to use it if the need arises.

Only silence greets me as I enter the desolate warehouse, its corridors stretching out before me, devoid of any signs of life or furniture gracing the barren floors. As I step farther into the place, a foul stench assaults my nostrils, making me gag as it weaves its way into my very marrow. The smell seeps from the walls like a festering wound, the rotten sensation emanating everywhere. Out of instinct, I grab my gun to keep it steady before me, my eyes searching for the office. Forcing myself to ignore the smell, I shift my focus to finding the schematics for the submarine and the shipment.

The heavy pitter-patter of rain against the windows resonates from the outside world, heightening my sense of urgency. After what feels like an eternity, I finally spot a door at the end of a smaller hallway, adorned with a sign that says, "Owner Only." A smirk plays on my lips as I approach, satisfied that the door is unlocked. I've reached the office—mission accomplished.

Instantly, I rummage through the drawers for any information I can find, all the while anxious about someone walking in. I'm acutely aware of the severe consequences the Grimaldi syndicate imposes on those who cross them, and they're not exactly known for being kind or merciful.

Beneath one of the drawers, I find a bundle of papers, my heart hammering against my ribcage as I take them out. Among them, one sheet appears torn, sending a surge of panic clawing through my senses as I scan the remaining text, wondering what valuable information once filled the page. *"Schedule—"* is written in bold, italicized letters on top of the paper, with nothing more.

A frustrated growl slips from my lips as annoyance takes over.

That can only mean one thing. Someone has either been here, or the Grimaldis have hidden it. I scan the room as if merely gazing at my surroundings will conjure the missing words into view. Glancing down at my phone, I've already connected it to the driver system I installed briefly in their security setup, granting me access to the hidden cameras scattered throughout the warehouse.

I deactivated the alarm for thirty minutes, and this current feed of the cameras will self-destruct when the alarm reactivates—leaving no trace of anyone having been here.

Filtering through the various viewpoints, I notice that no one is here. I try to tell myself that it's just nerves and paranoia, yet the mere presence of being here sends shivers down my spine, like spiders attempting to grab for me. It triggers a reaction that makes the inner child in me want to retreat into a corner, hide away forever, all because memories of the family I once had haunt my mind.

Scouring the room, determined to find the missing pages, I come up empty-handed. I consider other possible locations where the documents might be stashed—they were supposed to be here. Where else would anyone put schematics? But it seems as if they've been torn, indicating someone doesn't want the shipment details discovered.

Just as I'm about to leave the room, something odd catches my eye on my phone. The surveillance camera feed remains static. Some of them typically pivot back and forth, scanning the area with precision, but now they're as motionless as the rest. Squinting, I check the time stamps, noticing they're frozen at 11:12 p.m., three minutes prior to my arrival at the warehouse.

I put down my phone, standing utterly still while thoughts churn in my mind like a malfunctioning robot, gears grinding against each other in a chaotic mess. Realization dawns on me—they've been frozen all along. *That wasn't the plan.*

I instinctively tighten the grip around the gun, knuckles white from the motion. The hold gradually grows slick with sweat and the heat radiating from my trembling palms. Panic surges within me, like a prowling panther with its claws tearing at my sanity as it extinguishes the hunger.

I need to fucking focus and get out of here as soon as possible.

Opening the door to the office, I look left and right, scoping the area for any potential threats that might jump at me. Like before, it's silent. Almost eerily so. I push the thought aside, stepping out into the desolate hallways while aiming solely at the entrance.

I freeze in place the moment a visceral sensation courses through my veins like icy tendrils, fingers crawling down the nape of my neck. My limbs are frozen, every bone in my body motionless as I stare at the sight—a primal instinct telling me to run the other way and never look back, yet my curiosity gets the best of me.

My eyes widen in horror as I take in the scene before me, my pulse thudding loudly in my ears. Rivulets of blood glisten ominously in the darkened hallway, the only source of light filtering through the barred windows. They trace a macabre path leading toward a room I know serves as a refrigerator.

A lump forms in my throat, forcing me to swallow despite the sensation of nails scraping down my esophagus. The morbid crimson trail is fresh, marring the cold, gray floor while creating a stark contrast that makes my stomach churn with unease.

Following the bloodstains with the gun tightly clenched in my hand, I ensure it's loaded before arriving at the white, looming door. I know from scoping out the warehouse with the surveillance cameras in previous weeks that this refrigerator can only be opened from the outside.

A larger pool of scarlet liquid gathers outside the door, spreading with an impending sense of doom. My face turns a ghostly shade of pale as my eyes land on the blood smeared on the wall.

A fucking handprint.

A sickening feeling twists my insides while threatening to rise to my throat, and I realize how *unfit* I am for this kind of life. I never wanted to be part of this criminal world, but circumstances left me no choice.

Summoning what little resolve I have left, I push down the slick handle with my combat boot, refusing to touch it with my bare hands. The door reluctantly gives way to my efforts, its weight heavy against my shoulder as I push it open, not prepared for the horrors lying beyond.

There it is. A body nestled in a pool of blood with its skin retaining a warm hue reminiscent of life yet betraying the stillness of death. I zone in on his chest, searching in vain for the rise and fall of breath that animate the living. What did I expect?

I stare at the body, unable to comprehend why it's even there and how I could have missed it before. Unless it arrived moments ago, though if that were the case, wouldn't I have noticed something amiss?

A freezing horror grips me as my gaze follows the blood leading up to his bare torso, revealing a gaping wound serving as a canvas made of human flesh. My nails dig into my palms when I see the initials carved into his body, tearing through his skin in jagged slashes. They're raw, with initials unmistakably mine, made with cruelty hinting at malicious intentions.

A. V.

Shivers dance across my skin, leaving prickling sensations that make it feel as though the warehouse has been draped in a cold wind from the outside, despite being indoors. My teeth sink into my lip so fiercely that the familiar taste of metal floods my tongue. I scrutinize the body with my eyes, questions swirling like a tempest in my mind, wondering why the fuck my initials are carved into a corpse.

This is bad. Especially if the Grimaldis discover what the initials stand for, and who supposedly dared to carve them into one of their own. That the 'V' stands for Valenti—a name I was given by the family when the Grimaldis stripped me of theirs.

It could spell disaster, one I'm not ready to face all by myself.

I'm careful to avoid stepping into the crimson pools when I notice bold, red letters scrawled upon a crumbled piece of paper. It's smeared with the same liquid that stains the scene, as if the man before me died clutching it in his hand. Queasiness rises within me as I reluctantly step closer, bending down to retrieve the note, careful not to get blood on my hands. The putrid stench emanating from the already decaying body is overwhelming, and I stifle a gag.

All color drains from my face, leaving me a ghostly shade reminiscent of the dead when I realize who the note is meant for. Pulse thudding hard in my ears along with the rushing blood, it's hard to even concentrate on anything except that cryptic message.

Me.

Fucking hell.

"Arcane,

Your soul is as stained as mine, crumbling from the edges with the afterthought of decaying death. I've long awaited your return, hiding in the abyss of shadows. Keep your eyes open. The reaper will come for you, and he knows your name. Soon, you will enter a slow danse macabre."

A frown mars my eyebrows as I read the letter over again, attempting to decipher its meaning. There's no sender to indicate who wrote it, and the words are too puzzling. Yet, something is familiar about the handwriting, causing an eerie feeling to crawl over my skin.

With a pulsating headache tightening its grip on my skull, I unlock my phone with trembling hands the moment a sound shatters the silence. The phone nearly drops from my fingers, but I react just in time, grabbing it before realizing the sound came from the device in my hand.

With a sinking feeling in my stomach, I find that the surveillance camera program has been automatically launched, revealing a time stamp from twenty minutes ago, when I was still inside the office.

I'm rooted to the spot as I see a man in the video with an imposing frame that demands attention from any nearby soul, even through the screen. My breath quickens as I take in his overwhelming presence, and my gaze is drawn to the muscular posture on display beneath that leather jacket—broad shoulders accompanying it. His face is obscured by what appears to be a motorcycle helmet, shrouding his features in mystery.

He stares straight at the camera while a bloodied knife rests in his hand, tilting his head as his gaze seemingly pierces through the visor, through the screen, to lock onto mine.

Fear pulses through my veins like a drug, yet it all mingles with a tingling sensation deep within my core as I watch him. It's a confusing concoction, both terrifying and arousing, making me inwardly curse myself.

With no forewarning, his voice cuts through the panicked silence, echoing all around me despite the source being my phone. Sweet words laced with an undertone of anger. I'm trapped, even if he's not here—unable to move yet desperately needing to.

"Hello, little angel."

Chapter 6
Arcane

HIS WORDS ARE A relentless echo in my head, even now as I'm standing outside the warehouse, looking into the open space while checking if there are any stains left.

Turns out, disposing of a body is one fucking messy ordeal.

Blood littered the walls in every direction from the gruesome murder, not solely from the pools that formed around the body but also from the fresh trail left behind as I dragged it. Another telltale sign that could blow my cover and reveal someone has been here.

Two hours later, the blood has been bleached away, though the crimson stains my shirt and loose-fitting jeans. I'll be forced to burn them as soon as I get home to rid myself of all evidence.

Dragging my bare hand through my hair having discarded

the gloves—I realize my fingers are prickled with blood as well. *How did I even get blood in my hair?*

With a heavy sigh, I look back at the warehouse from the open garage door, its minimal interior stretching out before me, devoid of any signs of the corpse or gory scene I witnessed.

"I think we're done, yeah?" A deep voice comes from beside me, and I glance at Alec standing by the doorway to the warehouse.

His shirt clings to his chest with sweat, panting and huffing from the work of getting rid of a corpse. Said corpse is a fucking bulky guard as well, clad in a uniform adorned with the Grimaldis' emblem on the front.

I called Alec the moment the video feed stopped on my phone, erased without a trace. It dawned on me that whoever had been there, carving my initials into the body, possessed greater hacker skills than I. I've never gotten rid of a body before, so the first person I thought to call was Alec, although he wasn't very happy when he realized I went on this mission without Viper.

I know I can always count on Alec to show up when I need him to, and within ten minutes of calling, he was here, helping me clean up the bloody mess.

"I know you don't want to hear this, but it was fucking stupid of you to go against my father's orders like you did."

"You're right; I don't want to hear it."

I turn my back to Alec, but he grabs my wrist harshly. "I care about you, A, but you had one mission. Goddamn it. If my father finds out about this—"

"Then don't tell him," I cut him off, glaring into his eyes to emphasize my seriousness.

An ominous feeling settles over our surroundings as I stand inside the warehouse with Alec, and I know we'll have to leave soon if we want to avoid getting caught. It feels as if someone, somewhere, is watching me.

Could it be him? The man who carved my initials into the dead guard? The biker I've heard so much about? But why would he be here?

Because you've pissed him off, a voice chimes in my head.

"You know I can't lie to him," Alec says.

"Then ignore the subject."

"I know how mad he'll be, but I will be forced to tell him if you don't follow his orders."

"You don't even know half of the shit he has done to me." I shudder at the recollection of what Benjamin Valenti has put me through—ordering me to kneel, kiss his shoes, degrade myself for his liking. Rage overtakes me as I suppress the memories. "But I appreciate you not telling him."

Alec squeezes my shoulder, but there's something off in his expression—a coldness or calculation I can't quite place, as if he harbors secrets.

Casting one final look inside the warehouse, he begins his walk from the dock, and I greedily follow him, eager to leave the construction. The corpse is already rotting away in the trunk of his car, and I'm glad he'll be the one completely disposing of it.

After saying goodbye to Alec, I'm left alone, annoyed at not having received what I'd planned.

I can't help but feel that sense of being watched again, more prominent than before. It's as if the breeze of the wind reveals where this someone is, and I cast a glance over my shoulder once more, paranoid and searching through the darkness, revealing that indeed no one is there. It's only me and the vast expanse of the sea stretching out before me.

The wind picks up its pace, its weight bearing down on me, and the first drops of rain begin to fall, drowning the world in a shimmering glow and persuasive dampness. The unsettling feeling of being observed persists, but I attempt to ignore it, turning back to my bike, more than ready to leave this place behind.

I know that the initials carved into the guard was a warning, but from whom, I do not know. Tomorrow, I'll have to return to attempt to find the schematics once more. Deep in my bones, I feel that something isn't right, yet I cannot grasp the nature of this impending unease.

THE WIND HOWLS OUTSIDE, causing trees to scratch against the windows as if they are animals demanding to enter. I toss and turn in bed, unease trickling through me, only increasing with each passing second.

The image of the corpse with my initials carved into its flesh is seared into my mind, fueling my paranoia. I can't shake the feeling that evidence of us being there remains, that the Grimaldis will believe it was us who killed one of their guards.

My gaze is blurry as I look at the clock on my nightstand, the red text shining through the otherwise pitch-black room, showing that it's three a.m.

The drive home on my bike, usually exhilarating, lost its thrill in the rain. It felt like a storm had brushed over town, wind gusts making my bike sway at every curve, and the asphalt slippery from puddles. Throughout the ride, an eerie sensation of being watched gripped me, intensified by the unknown biker's cryptic message through the video feed. Despite driving alone in the middle of the night, it was as if I could hear the breaths of someone following, the distant revving of an engine trailing my bike.

With a deep breath, I glance at the clock, now revealing that it's three thirty a.m. The wind continues to brush against the apartment's window, branches knocking against the panes, only growing more violent. Through the curtains, I see the first strike of lightning splitting the sky with a silver glow, contrasting greatly with the blackened color of the night.

Soon after, thunder strikes, rumbling through the windows as if it's inside my bedroom. I hug the blanket closer to me, hating the fact that I'm still affected by the frightening sound of thunder. There's something about the thunder's intensity that always makes me unnerved, like a disconcerting echo. I take a deep breath to compose myself as a memory comes washing over.

"What are you so scared of?"

A deep grumble emanates through his throat as he stands in the doorway, his bare chest showcasing a chiseled, well-sculpted body. He casually props himself against the door, eyes meeting mine from across the room, with a smirk hinting at his lips.

Another roar from outside makes my body flinch as it splits the sky, feeling as if Thor is raging war against the clouds with his hammer. A pathetic squeak escapes me, causing my cheeks to redden, which he notices. The corner of his lips twitches, revealing an even bigger smirk.

With one step over the threshold, he comes closer before settling down beside me in bed. He puts his hand above mine, staring into my eyes with a glance that doesn't reveal his emotions.

Leaning closer, he whispers into the silence of the night. "Are you scared, little sister?"

"Don't mock me!" I exclaim, my cheeks flushing at the humiliation.

I don't want to seem weak or pathetic in front of the only person I look up to, a fifteen-year-old girl terrified of the rumbling sound of thunder. He brings his hand up to ruffle my hair, which only has me scowling at him, knowing how tangled it will be the next morning.

"I'm not." However, the smirk on his lips tells me otherwise.

Another ominous rumble rolls through the sky, but this time, it's a sharp, explosive clap that punctuates the atmosphere all around us. The intensity of the sound has my heart nearly breaking out of my ribcage, a faint panic taking on that I cannot get rid of. Without thought, my body moves closer to his. There's a twinkle in his eyes as he looks at me, shoulders subtly shaking from his chuckle. I hit his arm playfully, yet still rattled by the frightening sound.

"Stop it, Kaiden!"

"Okay, okay," he concedes.

Despite that, he still laughs at me, before his expression turns into a somber one when a louder, more vibrating and pulsating thunder explodes in the air.

Throughout the night, he holds my body close to his, my frame underneath the covers and his on top. He gently plays with my hair, allowing me to sleep while his husky yet soft voice drowns out the sound of thunder, hushing me into tranquility.

Gritting my teeth, I damn myself for the persistent memories of him that refuse to fade, despite the many years that have passed. It would be so much fucking easier if I could forget him. I'd rather do that, throw him and his haunting presence out of my mind before locking the gate to it, leaving him no possibility of ever entering again. If I could, I would erase his entire existence from my mind and past in the same way he destroyed me after promising to always be by my side.

The thunder roars again, and I decide to go grab a glass of water in the kitchen, knowing something cold will calm me down. Making my way to the kitchen, the quietness inside the apartment appears almost eerie, with the storm violently raging on the outside.

Right as I step foot inside the kitchen, goosebumps ripple across my skin, sending shivers down my spine and transforming the room into an instant ice world. The tension in the air thickens with my inability to breathe, and my eyes widen in response to the sight before me.

There's something on the window frame, a cryptic message that leaves me damn near gasping for breath.

What the fuck?

Written in what seems to be freshly formed fog is a message, as enigmatic as the one I encountered in the warehouse by the dock with the same handwriting. I swallow harshly, knives slicing through my throat.

"The reaper watches you when you sleep. You're as exquisite as a blood angel from hell."

Something is chilling about the words on the windowpane, as if someone has exhaled onto it. If I didn't know any better, I'd say the words came from within my kitchen.

That's impossible.

With deliberate steps, I approach the sink that is the closest to the window, and grab the gun from the kitchen drawer—tucked away in case of emergencies.

I'm not sure what I plan to do with it. It isn't as if I'll shoot through the glass if someone is outside, but the heavy weight in my hand is reassuring.

No one seems to be there.

With the gun still in hand, I return to my bedroom, forgetting what I'd intended to do in the kitchen.

As I'm about to lie down in bed, I notice the crimson droplets on top of my sheets, growing larger as I lift the blanket draping across them. Shock renders me motionless as I stare at the smeared blood, a contrast against the pristine fabric.

Frowning, I inspect myself for any signs of injury but find nothing at first, deepening my confusion.

I continue searching my body, standing in front of the full-length mirror on the other side of my room. Turning around, I look at my reflection, only to realize that I am indeed bleeding.

The frown marring my brow etches itself into my features as I discover a deep gash sliding across my shoulder blade to the front of my breast. Dried blood smears across my skin, evidence of the profuse bleeding. Despite the quantity of blood, the wound isn't deep. The adrenaline surging through me dulls the pain, but a lingering stinging sensation persists.

Suspicion gnaws at me, knowing I couldn't have inflicted it on myself while asleep, especially considering its clean, precise appearance, looking as if it was made by a sharper knife.

What the fuck is going on? Ever since I began preparing for this heist, mysterious things have happened. It's as if I'm descending into madness, my sanity slipping away once again.

Have the rivaling families found out about our little tryst and plans? Do they know about the USB drive I'm going to steal?

The lingering feeling of someone watching me remains.

Then, my phone pings with two incoming messages. One is an image, the other a text. My heart rate spikes up as I load the former, nearly bursting in half when the scene is displayed on the screen.

It appears to be a man clad in uniform, skin once vibrant yet now a pallid hue, draining away by the grip of solitude. Rigor mortis has settled in, leaving a stiffness in the limbs that are unyielding in an unnatural position. Nausea burns my throat as I look at the person, recognizing the carved flesh on his chest, the crooked letters *A. V.*

Hours later, his body appears more decayed, frozen in a position revealing a tortuous fate, skin wrinkling in death.

My eyes fixate on the Grimaldis' emblem, its letters a beacon, both inviting and dangerous, like a predator luring its prey in the night.

This can't be true. Alec got rid of the body.

Then why does it look as if it's at the Grimaldis' dock? I'd recognize that place anywhere—a place me and *him* used to play hide-and-seek when we were too bored with following our father around the dock while he dealt with shipments.

My breath constricts the moment I feel the trembling in my hands, opening the next message from the unknown sender—a warning that threatens to expose the entire heist and my involvement in it.

UNKNOWN: *Fail to meet me again, and the next thing you'll see is his severed head on their doorstep. Perhaps my little angel would like to be exposed to the wolves for her treachery instead. And you know damn well how malevolent the Grimaldis are.*

Chapter 7
Who Am I?
I guess you'll never know

EVEN IN THE DEAD of the night, I watch her. A silent shadow hiding amongst others, becoming one with the obscuring darkness slowly seeping through my corrupted soul, silently waiting for the right moment to strike so I can take and conquer.

Soon, it's my time to finally own her soul and mind completely.

She's a pawn in a game beyond our godforsaken town's comprehension, oblivious to the looming danger and the horrors unfolding behind her, hiding in the shadows much like myself. Yet, unlike me, those horrors are veiled behind a theater curtain, as if this were merely a staged play captivating the public.

The unsettling problem is that *no one* fucking comprehends the full magnitude of Penumbra Crest, and the insidious corruption embedded within the five ruling families. Once, I might have cared about the innocent civilians caught amidst the crossfire, but now? I couldn't care less, not after so many people lied to me. Countless articles have fabricated tales about me, spewing bullshit unworthy of my attention.

I might be ruthless with no fucks to give, but I'm not heartless.

The night is beautifully laid before me like a secret whisper sending soothing words of tranquility. The moon hangs in the sky, casting its silver-like glow through the windows and enveloping the room in scattered shadows.

Hidden in the shadows, I fixate on her slumbering form—so beautiful yet so tainted and twisted. She's got spunk in her, evident in how she punctured the tire of my bike a while back when I was merely observing her from afar. I can't deny that witnessing her vulnerability didn't stir something primal within me, waking my cock to life from the sheer violence.

Her platinum locks cascade over the pillow beside her, framing her face as she rests on her stomach, arms hugging the pillow beneath her head. One arm holds a tattoo of a butterfly splattered in water while simultaneously drowning in it.

I allow my gaze to roam her form, every curve and contour calling to my desire. Clad in nothing but an oversized T-shirt, her figure is both alluring and achingly exposed, the fabric riddled up against her stomach and revealing her little panties.

Approaching the bed where she lies, my hand involuntarily reaches out to stroke her cheek. She stirs but does not awaken.

A side glance toward the nightstand reveals the empty glass, its contents fully drained. My deed went unnoticed, the sleeping pill seamlessly dissolving in the water to erase all evidence.

She's so easy to hurt like this, and the need to mark her as mine thrums through me like the deadliest drug, ready to consume every rational thought. With a knife in my leather-gloved hand, I trace a delicate line along her shoulder, pressing just enough to break the surface of her vulnerable skin. The sharp sting of the blade draws forth a crimson shade that makes desire flood my veins. Serves her right for puncturing my R1 bike. A hiss escapes between gritted teeth as the agonizing arousal coils deep within me. With my free hand, I apply pressure to the throbbing outline of my cock, squeezing painfully hard.

The need to inflict more pain makes me push the knife deeper into her skin, slicing a straight line, not enough to scar permanently but deep enough to coax forth trickles of blood down her shoulder blade. It's intoxicating to observe how it smears her back, leaving her so fucking vulnerable and at my mercy.

Satisfaction floods my being, and I feel my cock pressing against the zipper of my jeans. She whimpers softly in her sleep, eyes fluttering, but she remains oblivious to what I'm up to. The arousal pulsating through my soul is barely manageable anymore, forcing me to take action as I put the knife in my pocket before swiftly unzipping my pants to take out my cock. A groan escapes my lips as I stroke the hardened length, watching her sleeping so peacefully like a little lamb, unaware of the predator beside her.

With each movement of my hand, a rush of euphoria floods my senses while I grit my teeth, taking in every curve and those goddamn panties. Carefully, I grab the hem of the fabric, slowly dragging it down her legs. I can't help but fist her panties around my cock, my hips instinctively rocking against my hand. *Fuck.* My imagination runs wild, thinking about all the ways I want to devour her.

But it's not time yet—not until she learns about who I am, and about the predator lurking beneath the surface, waiting to own her.

She will wish she never met me while kneeling before me, submitting to the one predator she never should have surrendered to.

A smirk spreads on my lips, soon overtaking my pleasure as I continue stroking my dick, craving the pain mixed with pleasure. I'm thrusting my cock into the panties wrapped around it, rocking my hips faster as my balls tighten with the need to come. With one look down at the blood I drew from her flesh, I picture her spread open, at my mercy and begging me to save her. But I won't. Oh, how I wouldn't save her.

Her scent envelops the space, and I inhale it, only now acknowledging how comforting it feels. That coupled with the sensation of her panties wrapped tightly around my throbbing length has me pumping my cock even harder. Soon, pleasure wreaks havoc over me, plunging me over the edge of madness as I come in her panties, ensuring that the fabric absorbs every drop.

I'm a little breathless by the time I'm done, not fully satisfied yet knowing I have to get going.

There's a little devil awaiting punishment, and I thrive in the anticipation of the fear I'll instill.

Discarding her panties in a secluded corner, far away from her unsuspecting gaze, I slip through the unlocked window and meld into the shadows once more, biding my time until the effects of her sleeping pills in her system wear off.

———

TREES SURROUND ME AS I stare at her delicate figure standing in the kitchen, biting her lip with a determined expression that instantly sends fire roaring through my veins, raging and fighting the urges within the beast inside me. My gaze fixates on her with such intensity that I half expect the window to explode into hundreds of broken shards under the weight of my piercing glare.

Her eyes, a unique blend of azure and cobalt, reminiscent of a tranquil ocean, hold flickers of warmth that transform into a fit of raging anger, coursing through the nerves zipping through my brain.

The ebb and flow of emotions within those orbs create a mesmerizing dance, and as her gaze falls upon the windowpane, her face visibly drains of color. A delicately, vulnerable hue that makes my blood scorching hot, fighting the urge to break inside her apartment once again, if only to feel those very eyes bestow upon me.

Such a beautiful, fucking delicate thing, terrified of the words written on the glass.

She's a deer caught in the headlights on the Autobahn, needing to flee but unable to. If they freeze, the predators won't see them, right? But that's all wrong. There is no saving those deer on the road, nor is there any saving *her* from *me*.

There never was. Especially not now when I've gotten my chance to see the blood trickle from her and feel her close to me.

She comes closer to the window, her short platinum hair brushing against her shoulders. Everything about her draws me in, like a moth to a flame.

Her figure defies the ideals in this world, and that's exactly what makes her so irresistible, from her not-so-flat stomach to her thighs and generous curves. Her face, devoid of any makeup, is beautiful no matter the flaws, and the lines in her face are a masterpiece waiting to be explored. She stands at my height, eye to eye, at five feet ten inches.

Observing her leaves a physical craving within my body, making me unable to move, transfixed by her sheer aura. The terror is evident on her face, and a smile stretches my lips as I observe her. She's completely oblivious to the fact that I'm out here, staring at her, having been following her for days.

Having her panties wrapped around my cock.

Despite being an intelligent woman, she sure as fuck isn't very smart when it comes to her own safety. It infuriates me to see her overlook potential threats, knowing that other predators can zone in on her, stealing what's *mine*.

Now, she's looking out the window, obviously not seeing anything, which has her turning her back to me with a small huff that makes her eyebrows scrunch.

Cute.

Making my way through the trees, I round the corner to get a better view of her when she enters her bedroom again. Through the creaks in the curtain, I notice her unsteady legs, trembling with the fright that must be paralyzing her.

I'm once again hidden away in the darkness, not ready to reveal myself to her just yet. A thunder rumbles through the sky which has her figure tensing in distress. Personally, I fucking love the mayhem and chaos that comes with nature's eruption in the sky.

She stands before the mirror, taking in her appearance. The beautiful slice marring her flesh, creating a crimson hue of something wonderful, meets my gaze as I look in the mirror's reflection along with her. She still doesn't know that I'm here, and that makes something spark within me, a potent desire and yearning to hold her and have her close to me again. The need is so overwhelming that it feels as if my insides are on the verge of tearing apart, consumed by a torrent of visceral sensations, and I feel my cock twitching. Touching myself in her presence was far from enough.

I retrieve the knife tucked into my jacket pocket, feeling its weight in my leather-gloved hand. My gaze locks onto the crimson liquid gleaming across the silver surface, and I find myself fixated, consumed by an obsession. I crave her fucking blood and agony like a parched wanderer seeking an oasis in the desert.

Why didn't she obey the orders to meet me? Anger seeps through my bones at the thought of it, and I cling to the memory of her whimpering in her sleep as I let my knife glide against her back. The mere thought satiates my thirst, the same torrent of emotions erupting inside me like an active volcano.

For too fucking long I've wanted her, watched her from the shadows.

Now, it's finally time for retribution.

I grab my phone, sending her the image of the corpse I found lying in the Valentis' truck. I've had my eyes on them for years, ever since they took her in.

Satisfaction grates through every cell in my body as I remember the thrill I got from Arcane's fear when she saw the guard's body in the refrigerator room.

Her body visibly stiffens as she stands in her room, shoulders rising, and I know that if she held something in her hand, it would clatter to the floor. Her uncertain gaze is locked on the phone as I send my next message—a warning and threat for daring to defy me.

For that alone, she deserves to be punished, but not in the way I usually punish my prey. No, she deserves something that will leave her begging for mercy, with hands tied behind her back and my cock deep in her throat until tears slip down her cheeks.

Fuck. The fantasy has my cock hardening once more.

I can practically feel the anger intermingled with the fear that courses through her.

With one final glance at her figure, I lick her blood off my knife, loving the sweet taste of her, before I turn away and enter the shadows into the unknown.

Until the reaper and his victim cross paths once more.

Chapter 8
Arcane

19 years old

MY EARLIEST MEMORY IS that of utter darkness, a vast expanse where emptiness weighed heavily on me like a stone. I used to believe I was born into that obscurity, enveloped so completely that I became one with it. My tattered room back at the orphanage was my sanctuary; I'd huddle beneath the sheets, yearning for all the bad to seep away.

It never did, but with time, I learned to adapt.

At nine, Kaiden entered the orphanage after losing his only living parent. He became my sole companion, and despite carrying his own burdens, he was a beacon in the void, saving me from myself countless times. Two years later, a couple sought to adopt a young boy to raise as the heir to their business empire.

They found Kaiden, but he refused to leave me behind. Since we'd become inseparable, Mr. and Mrs. Grimaldi had no choice but to adopt me too.

Kaiden and I only grew closer over the years, our bond deepening to the point of obsession. But wasn't it normal for siblings to share such an intense connection?

During stormy nights, when the thunder rolled through the sky, he'd sneak into my room through the slippery balcony, holding me close. Sometimes, we'd intertwine our fingers, seeking solace in each other's touches. Other times, we'd merely lie together.

But as time passed, his possessiveness over me only intensified, his mood worsening along with the bruises as he spent more time with our dad and his shady business.

Ever since he did those things a year ago during our hide-and-seek game in the forest clearing, I've found it impossible to maintain a normal sisterly demeanor. He always makes me blush, stirring a tempest of emotions within me, leaving my hormones in disarray.

That's why I have to keep my distance—I can't be near him without feeling all hot and flustered, my mind consumed by memories of that time. The physical response he evokes in me still leaves me breathless, my panties drenched with uncontrollable arousal from the intensity of his gaze.

I'm startled by the approaching footsteps, sending my heart jumping inside my ribcage. A woman clad in a uniform enters, the clicking of her high heels reverberating through the marble walls. Her hair is pulled back into a tight bun as she fixes me with a disapproving glare.

"What's wrong with you lately?" Mom asks as she steps beside me where I sit by the kitchen island, staring down at my bitten nails.

How could I possibly tell her what's wrong? *Every. Fucking. Thing.*

I meet her gaze, noting the charcoal accents around her eyes and the tint of blush on her cheeks—her makeup is impeccable. The Grimaldis don't accept anything less than perfection.

"She's just her usual grumpy self." Kaiden's voice echoes from the doorway as he enters the kitchen in just a pair of pants.

His chiseled, well-defined body is on full display, showcasing those muscles he always works so hard on, and I nearly choke on my saliva as I take in the sight of him. He's a perfect wonder, and he fucking knows it. With blond hair looking like honey in the sunlight, he sports a calculated grin that would make any person fall for him. A sour taste lingers in my mouth as I avert my gaze, hating the fact that he's my brother.

It's been a couple of months since I turned nineteen, and the intensity with Kaiden has only grown. He's a menace existing in the same place as me, making me squirm everywhere I go.

Is it normal to feel such maddening lust for your foster brother?

The sour taste in my mouth becomes worse as Kaiden smirks at me, his gaze piercing through mine. I need to get out of here. I can't breathe, can't think, can't fucking exist when he's near. I feel like I'm going to drown any second, and there's no hope of saving me.

Mom's voice snaps me back to the present. "There's a gala we have to attend tomorrow," she announces with a firm tone. "You both must attend. The other four powerful families of Penumbra Crest will be there, and we have to uphold the utmost respect and status."

Each word is lodged in my windpipe while threatening to choke me if I dare speak back.

I need to get out of here.

"Of course," I mutter absentmindedly, heading toward the hallway.

All I can think about is the desperate need to escape his presence. He drives me to the point of madness without even realizing it, and I need to gather my thoughts. Quietly slipping out of the manor, I grab Mom's car keys despite not having a driver's license. I wasn't allowed one like Kaiden, but that didn't prevent me from sneaking out and teaching myself to drive with a friend from school.

There aren't many police patrolling the affluent areas of town, especially not at this hour. Even if I were caught, my parents would easily buy me out of trouble, though their disappointment would be my price to pay.

Setting the car in drive, I leave the dark front yard, grateful for the quiet hum of the electric engine. Hopefully, Mom won't even notice that I took her car, given the vastness of the manor.

After twenty minutes of driving, I reach a deserted gas station.

It's the perfect place to be alone, away from this overwhelming feeling that evades my every thought and emotion—even if it's a bit odd to bring an electric car to a gas station.

Parking somewhat haphazardly, I step out onto the concrete pavement, the cool night air brushing over me.

A single light keeps the station illuminated, casting a shimmer that accentuates the desolation. Most people are nestled in their beds by now, preparing for the demands of the next day, whether it be school or work. I can't bear to care.

With a sigh, I lean against the car's hood, scanning the deserted surroundings. A prickling sensation grabs me, like pins and needles spreading over my body, alerting me that someone is nearby. The wind whispers through the night, the only other audible sound besides my breathing. Straining my ears, I search for any sign of movement, but the gas station remains eerily still.

No other vehicles occupy the station, and instead of the peaceful solitude I sought, I'm now enveloped in a chilling atmosphere thick with tension, setting my nerves on edge. A rustling sound breaks the silence, and I jolt in alarm as I attempt to locate the source. No one is close by, and regret gnaws at me for ever having left the manor.

Paranoia grips me with cold fingers as another sound startles me, this time from my phone vibrating. Trying to catch my breath, I tremble as I reply, my lungs craving oxygen.

"Hello?" I utter, casting an eye over my shoulder.

Somewhere in the distance, the sound of crickets blends with

the stirring wind, but there's only silence from the other end—
until a deep breath breaks it. A single one, followed by nothing
more. Seconds drag on, my apprehension escalating until a voice
emerges from the speaker—a quiet, dark one.

"The reaper is here," it whispers before the call abruptly ends.

With my heart lodged in my throat, I quickly make my
way inside the gas station. The eerie feeling of being watched
accompanies me, every step echoing ominously against the
pavement.

Once inside, I dare breathe a sigh of relief, greeted by the
friendly cashier whose name tag reads "Dom." He appears to be
in his twenties with a smile revealing charming dimples. I browse
the shelves, selecting snacks and a drink, before approaching the
checkout.

Dom strikes up a conversation, a welcome distraction from the
previous tension. Despite the lingering unease in the back of my
mind, I relax ever so slightly in his presence.

"Nice to meet you…?" he prompts for my name.

"Arcane," I respond, offering a friendly smile.

"Arcane," he repeats, nodding in acknowledgment. "Hope to
see you soon," he adds playfully, his demeanor flirty and cheerful.

With a nod and a faint smile, I gather my purchases and head
back to the car. The brief encounter with Dom eased some of the
tension from the strange phone call earlier, especially those cryptic
words uttered.

I settle into the driver's seat, unprepared for the warning signals blaring within my mind. Before I can even reach for the car key, a rough leather-gloved hand clamps around my throat, its texture scraping against my skin. Chains bite into my flesh, yanking my head back to the headrest and restricting the oxygen entering my lungs.

Panic surges within me as I struggle frantically against the restraints, but it's in vain. My eyes widen, horror piercing every fiber of my being as the lack of oxygen makes the car spin. It's a cruel realization that I forgot to lock the car door when I entered the store.

I claw at the chains, nails scraping futilely against the metal as I try with all my might to break free.

A dark, amused chuckle fills the air behind me, freezing me in confusion. "Did you think you could run from me? Avoid your big brother like the bad little sister you are?" A growl follows the words.

It's a strange concoction—arousal mingling with fear in a dizzying whirlwind, every nerve caught in a dance of conflicting emotions. My mind reels with the realization of who is behind me in the car.

The chains dig into my skin, allowing me to breathe but restricting my movements. I turn to look behind me, but he tightens his grip on the chains to prevent me from doing so.

"No looking, sister. You're mine for the taking."

"Kai—Kaiden?" I stammer, my words laced with confusion. He continues choking me with the chains, and there's nothing else I can do but accept defeat, even as my heart pounds like a madman in a desperate plea to break free. "What are you doing here?"

"Don't you think I see how much I affect you? How much you squirm in my presence?" His deep chuckle rumbles through the crowded space of the car, sending goosebumps spreading across my skin.

I gulp in lungfuls of air, apprehension gripping me at the dangers of the moment.

Beneath the fear, something dark flutters in my stomach, causing me to squeeze my thighs together in a somewhat embarrassing reaction. The arousal of having my oxygen cut off, especially with him behind me, mingles with the fear and creates a tumultuous mix of emotions that make me struggle once more.

"Get off me, Kaiden," I warn as the hand not holding the chains trail from my neck to the dip between my breasts. I bite my tongue to keep from making a sound, annoyance and something primal flickering inside me.

How fucking dare he come here and scare me like this? Holding me captive like this?

I can't help but shudder as his hand finds its way below my shirt, under my bra, lightly twisting my nipple. The metallic tang of blood spreads on my tongue as I bite down on my lip.

"Escaping from home, stealing Mom's car," he muses, hand kneading one breast. "All to get away from your big brother. Was it to flirt with that cashier, huh? Or was it something else?"

Though I can't see him, I catch his eyes in the rearview mirror, nearly glowing from the single light illuminating the car. He holds a lethal glint as he meets my gaze, causing me to gulp down my nervousness.

"You can't hide from me."

His hand slides from my breast to the other, kneading it with the chain still around my neck, restricting my movements. I'm rendered powerless as a sharp intake of breath escapes me as he pinches my nipple, sending a jolt of sensations through my body. His touch dips even lower, inching closer to my thighs as his hand slides over my stomach and hips. I buckle against the seat in a pathetic attempt to escape, but it's fruitless as his hand meets the outside of my clit, and I'm unable to restrict the gasp from slipping out of me.

His eyes are dazed in the rearview mirror, a presence like the darkest archdemon ready to purge my soul. "I bet if I told you to bend over to the other seat, ass up in the air, I'd see your arousal dripping from your sweet cunt." There's a predatory edge to his tone, and my stomach flutters harshly, wild insects slicing me from the inside out.

I bite back the need to whimper as his hand continues its exploration down my body, touching me in ways he has never touched me before, circling over the fabric of my panties and my clit. He's making me disoriented, and I hate the fact that I don't mind it. Fear and desire coil in me, and I'm unable to figure out any of my thoughts.

"Kaiden, we can't do this," I whisper, knowing how futile my words are. He won't stop; a predator never stops when it has set its sights on its prey.

"You're not the one in charge now, little sister. You're going to listen to your big brother like the good innocent girl I know you are, and you're going to climb over here," he demands, leaving me paralyzed with indecision. I'm frozen in time as if my brain is short-circuiting.

When I don't instantly follow his orders, he grabs the chain harder around my throat, making me stutter on my breath. With one swift movement, he leans toward the side and grabs me, lifting me like a rag doll until I'm in the back seat with him. My knees scrape against the other seats.

"What the fuck?" I exclaim, but he ignores me.

"Bend over," he growls, and I don't listen to him. "Bend over, *brat*," he repeats.

A sharp, stinging sensation comes from my right ass cheek, burning and twisting as I realize he spanked me. Another one, until I feel my legs wanting to clench from the unnerving arousal.

"Hands on each front seat and spread your legs. I can practically smell how much you want it."

I do as he says, not thinking over my decision. Everything changes here. Every-fucking-thing, and I feel drunk on emotions, unable to fully comprehend the situation.

My nerves tingle with anticipation and fear, knowing how taboo this is. Knowing how fucked and twisted I am for *wanting* this.

He pushes my hips against him, and I still the moment I feel his hard cock pressing against my ass.

I attempt to speak, but he stuffs the chain into my mouth, the metallic taste overwhelming my senses. I'm prevented from speaking as the cold material meets my tongue.

This can't possibly be happening.

But it is.

His erection pressing against me feels like confirmation, but I refuse to believe it. I'm his goddamn sister.

Nails grip my hips, and I can't help but grind against him, arousal coating my panties despite the revulsion.

It's sickening. Fucking sick.

I can't see him behind me in the back seat, but I feel his hands as he slides down my pants. I'm too stunned to reply.

Without warning, his fingers find their way between my legs, teasing and touching my folds, igniting a roaring fire in me. I'm terrified of what this will mean for us, but I'm unable to stop him as he expertly works my clit, circling it. Moaning around the chains, I'm powerless as he plunges two fingers inside me, pushing me forward until I'm draped over the center console, near the gear lever.

The sound of his belt unbuckling sends shivers down my spine, and I close my eyes, bracing myself for what's to come.

He prods himself against my entrance, cock sliding over my clit, eliciting a torrent of desire. I'm already soaking him, even before he pushes inside me. Leaning over me, he kneels beside me in the cramped car, his tall and muscular frame almost too large for the limited space.

He releases the chain, and it rattles as it lands below me, grazing my nipples and causing me to gasp.

"I know you've never fucked someone before," he whispers in my ear, and I blush before annoyance comes over me.

"And how do you know that?"

"I've been watching you. Keeping track."

Yet again, I'm too stunned to speak.

"Relax, baby. You will take my cock, and you're going to love how I feel inside you. You'll remember exactly who you belong to."

I whimper around his length, overwhelmed by the enormity of him as he enters me fully.

"I don't belong to anyone," I breathe out.

"Oh, angel. We both know that's a lie."

I'm sore, and for just a fraction of a second, he allows me to adjust to his size. His gentleness is shocking, and soon, pleasure wreaks through me in electric shock waves. I'm clenching around his cock, hips rocking into mine as I lay helplessly over the center console, unable to move an inch yet loving it all the same.

"We shouldn't be doing this," I manage to moan between breaths.

"Shouldn't and can't are two different words," he counters, his grip on my short hair tightening as he thrusts deeper, becoming more violent with each thrust.

"And I'm not feeling particularly kind today. You did something very fucking bad, Arcane. Now, you will come around my cock and milk me dry until I spill everything inside you." *Thrust.* "My cum will trickle down your legs when you get home. I'm going to corrupt you and your thoughts."

His words send a jolt through me, and tightness builds in my core when I'm unable to resist the coming wave of pleasure as my orgasm nears. This is too intense, too fucking forbidden. It feels as if I might shatter into pieces.

He coaxes a release from me as his fingers slip into my mouth mid-moan, hitting the back of my throat until I'm gagging, saliva dripping down the sides. The sounds he makes are beautiful, heavenly, and utterly too erotic as sweat coats our bodies.

The car rocks violently with each powerful thrust, and he pushes me toward my release. Another spank echoes around us as his palm meets my ass cheek while thrusting his fingers deeper until I gag again, feeling as if I might puke.

"Don't ever fucking flirt with another man again," he growls.

I'm soaked with arousal as I coat his cock with my slickness, my nipples two hardened buds beneath my T-shirt.

"You think I won't get what I want? You think I'll ever let you have any other man? You're mistaken. You're mine now, and in all the lifetimes to come."

I come, screaming out my release as my entire body trembles. I'm falling, fucking tumbling toward the end of the earth as I reach the edge of ecstasy, gagging around his fingers before they leave my mouth.

With a groan, he thrusts deeper into me before spilling inside, filling me up so deep. I've never felt anything like this before.

We just fucked inside our mom's car.

"Don't think for a moment I won't kill any other man who dares look at you."

Dread thrums through me as I'm shaken by the creeping sensation that this is all a part of a twisted game.

But the next day, the news flashes across the television.

Dom West took his own life with a gun.

Yet, I can't shake the feeling that Kaiden had something to do with it.

Chapter 9
Arcane
Present Day

AN UNEASY FEELING LINGERS in me the entire morning after, chilling me to my very core. I shift in my seat as I meet the lethal gaze of Benjamin Valenti across the room, feeling like an insect being scrutinized under a magnifying glass, like being prodded and poked by tools that could kill me.

Alec is to my right, with Antonio beside Benjamin. The tension is thick in the room, with everyone on edge.

For seconds, I'm observed by Mr. Valenti as he merely stares at me with those hardened eyes and lips formed into a straight line. He doesn't look satisfied at all.

Merely remembering the night before has left me rattled, shaken like a leaf consumed by a strong gale. Throughout the ride, it was as if a weighted stone pressed against my lungs, attempting to steal all my oxygen. Almost as if a hand reached inside my ribcage, grabbing hold of the organs beneath before ripping them out.

Now, it's like a distant memory, and I can't even begin to fathom if it was reality or a dream, though the bandage around my shoulder blade hints at the truth—that someone was inside my apartment as I was asleep.

Not someone.

Him.

The biker.

Viper García.

He's the only one I was supposed to meet. Did he kill the guard, stealing the corpse, only to threaten to reveal it all to the Grimaldis? It'd put the whole heist in danger.

Clearing his throat, Mr. Valenti eventually comes closer to both Alec and me, settling into an office chair among the many lined around the conference table. I've always despised being near him, memories from years I'd rather forget washing up in my mind like sand along the shore.

"Get on your knees and kiss my shoes if you want me to show mercy," Antonio growls, his striking brown eyes narrowing down on me. Running his fingers through his brown hair, now peppered with gray, showing his age, he exchanges a look with Mr. Valenti. They both share the same kind of glance before inching even closer, and I have no other choice but to comply, lowering myself down on the ground.

A surge of bile rises in my throat at the thought of that first year when they exploited my body for what they deemed the greater good. It was all bait to capture my attention and manipulate my desire for my well-deserved revenge. I wonder if Alec even knows what a fucking pervert his father and his second-in-command is.

I lift my gaze, noticing how close Mr. Valenti is—close enough for the scent of his expensive cologne to envelop me.

"We only have a few more preparations to make before we can proceed with the heist, but the time is running out. The other organizations are directing their attention on this matter, assuming we're building up for war after they've seen us—" His eyes flicker to mine. "—*You*, driving around their lands."

His words have rage boiling within me, hating that he insinuates something from merely a false observation.

"Do you think you're capable of executing such a complicated heist, Arcane?"

His words catch me off guard, so cold and uncaring with no hint of emotion to them. It's as if he doesn't care whether or not he crushes me from the inside with the words he just spoke. He only wants to hurt me in the same way everyone has always hurt me. Betrayed and ruined me.

Clenching my fists, I tilt my head up in a show of defiance. "Yes, of course."

I barely even recognize my voice, gritting out the words. He fucking knows that this heist is my chance to finally get the revenge I've sought out since I was abandoned by the Grimaldis, left to fend for myself because of *him*. Because they only wanted Kaiden, and I was the baggage.

How fucking dare he?

Acknowledging the fact that I'll only make matters worse should I talk back, I opt to sit my ass on the chair while giving him a feigned sweet smile. "I won't disappoint you."

Nausea grips me, turning my stomach inside out as the urge to gag rises. Swiftly, I swallow down a mouthful of saliva, desperate to conceal the disgust welling up within me from those words.

"I'll hold you to your word," he declares, a glint in his eyes underscoring the implicit threat. "I expect you to work with Viper García and find out everything he knows about this. Or else this entire heist will be ripped out of your hands, much like I'll rip your heart out if you don't fall in line, *girl.*" With such venom, he spews out the last word, leaving me half expecting a snake's tongue to lurk within his mouth.

He strides out of the conference room with Antonio in tow, as well as his closest personal guard. I have to restrain myself from going after him and lashing out all of my annoyance against his face, crushing it underneath my already bruised knuckles.

Too fucking bad I have to play the dutiful part of a submissive woman, lowering to her knees for men whenever they tell her to, obeying their every command if only to protect my own life. That is how it works in our world, dominated by men who have all the power the Devil gifted them, leaving us women alone in the shadows, constantly fighting for our time to shine.

"Are you okay?" Alec asks me, his voice laced with concern.

I force a smile, attempting to brush off the annoyance stirred by his despicable father. Alec squeezes my uninjured shoulder.

It appears my only chance for vengeance lies in aligning myself with the one man I've avoided like the plague.

"We're getting the sonar equipment today," he merely states, shifting my attention from the floor up to his eyes. I nod, hoping everything will go well with that mission.

Before diving into the depths of the main heist, a myriad of preparations needs to be done. We're halfway there, with the impending doomsday looming so closely—on the third of July. Two weeks stand between us and the robbery that will reshape it all. I steel myself, anchoring my resolve to that knowledge of how little time is left. I can hold on for that long.

I have to.

Only then will I finally let go of this clawing agony shredding me apart with each passing day, reclaiming justice against those who ruined my life and future, who relished in the twisted desire of seeing me fail in this man-made world.

It's a bitter irony that I can't get my revenge on *him*. The very man who obliterated everything I held dear, simultaneously destroying me from the inside out.

WINDING ALONG THE COASTAL bends, I'm offered a glimpse

of the distant horizon hiding far off in the sea. The visor on my helmet tints the outside world, and the salty breeze of the ocean carries through the air, providing a soothing touch. Navigating carefully around the weathered asphalt patches and cracks, I finally reach the dock.

The closer I come to the roads I recognize, the more I want to retch until nothing is left in my emptied stomach. The familiar lands of the place I once used to visit with my foster father and brother loom before me, the building smaller than what I remember.

Slowing my speed, memories assault me of the time they allowed my curious, naive self to learn the family business. It was a time in my life when I viewed the world with optimism, full of possibilities and dreams that were quickly snuffed out overnight. That day unfolded into a nightmare, and I vividly recall the unsettling touch of an older fisherman's greasy fingers violating me in the building's hallway, trapping me with his intrusive hand on my waist. That day ended with my brother sporting a black eye from our father's wrath. In my room late at night, he told me the bruises were worth it because he'd hurt the fisherman for touching me.

Willing away the memories, I park my bike, needing to survey the area before venturing farther. My priority lies in stealing the sonar equipment, confirmed by Alec to exist here, and to uncover what happened to the submarine's schematics. It's a risky mission as the Grimaldis always have been known for their tight security on their biggest platforms—this dock.

Waves crash against the bridge far off in the distance—a sound that has become familiar with the numerous scoping missions I've been on. Now, we're finally one step closer to stealing the car with the USB drive from the incoming submarine.

Moving silently, I remain on high alert as I glance over my shoulder in case anyone's following. Dusk gradually closes in, orange and pink hues painting the sky in a beautiful view that takes my breath away.

High gates loom before me, leading into the area itself, with barbed wire on top to prevent strangers from entering. The instance I come closer, an ominous feeling settles deep within me. Beckoning me closer, screaming inside my soul that something is wrong. The gates are supposed to be closed, not open.

The Grimaldi syndicate guards their secrets with utmost secrecy, except I've mastered the art of outsmarting their intricate safety systems, thanks to the Valenti family. If all had gone according to my plan, the Grimaldis would've closed their gates and I would have been the one to silently open them. Yet, here they stand ajar. A surge of suspicion rises deep within me as I approach the gates, every nerve tingling as my muscles lock.

A heavy sense of foreboding settles in my gut, sending warnings to my brain. With caution, I retrieve the gun from my pocket, holding it discreetly, prepared for any threat that may arise. All the while, I maintain an innocent appearance, ensuring I appear unarmed.

The moment I'm about to enter the dock, my phone vibrates. Frowning, and a little annoyed at the thought that it might be Alec disturbing me, I open it. My pulse thuds harshly in my ears as I read the message over again, fear coiling around me like a vise.

UNKNOWN: *I left you a little gift.*

There's nothing more than that, only those six words from an unknown sender, making icy fingers roam over me until I'm shuddering.

ARCANE: *Who the fuck is this?*

After a minute, there's still no reply, which leaves me staring at my phone with simmering hatred, as if it has committed the worst crime. Each passing second makes me feel more dumbfounded as I merely stand and wait for a reply that likely won't come.

A prickling feeling at the nape of my neck distracts me from the phone, and I'm suddenly aware that I'm no longer alone. Despite the instinctive urge to tense, I force myself to relax, refusing to show any sign of awareness of the presence nearby.

I enter the dock's perimeters, gazing at the darkening sky providing little illumination to the path ahead. Lampposts are stationed outside the massive building, casting an eerie glow on my surroundings, making this all the more menacing.

All my steps are deliberate, the churning in my stomach intensifying tenfold. A haunting tune of the wind in the distance carries me further. But, when I'm just about to turn left around the corner of a container positioned inside the gates, I feel something wet beneath my foot.

It's slippery, adhering to my sneakers and transforming the asphalt into an odd substance. With a mix of horror and fascination, I stare down at the ground, half convinced I've stepped into pee or some shit like that.

What I never expected was to see a crimson hue coloring the underside of my shoe, the light from the lamppost faintly illuminating the liquid splattered across the asphalt. Yet, it's not splattered; it's gathered in a pool as if someone has bled out here. I swallow harshly, feeling the molten lava traveling down my throat in an attempt to scorch me alive.

My hand is steadily placed inside my pocket, gripping for the gun there, as my ears are perked to hear the slightest sound that could reveal whatever is around me.

This is too easy. It shouldn't be this easy to enter their dock and scope it out, and yet it's as if I have free rein to the entire area.

Where is everyone?

With another cautious step forward, the slickness of the asphalt becomes unmistakable, and I lower my gaze in bewilderment. What I witness next sends my heart racing faster than a speeding car on the road, harder than thunder rumbling through the skies. It's dull, painful, and sucks the oxygen from my lungs despite my attempts to maintain a calm, steady breathing.

Only inches away lies a gruesome discovery. A hand soaked in blood that has long since dried into the skin. The lamp's feeble light casts shadows, revealing not only the hand but the arm also. I barely dare look further, feeling utterly vulnerable in the dock of the family that once betrayed me.

Returning my gaze to the gory sight, I notice that the horror doesn't end with the severed limb. Bile rises in my throat, leaving a sour aftertaste as I see the rest of the body, chest torn apart as if slashed and ripped open with the sharpest blade. I've witnessed plenty of blood in my life, yet this ghastly moment triggers nausea threatening to empty my stomach.

This is more than some mere murder; it's personal.

The unsettling feeling of being watched heightens, as if a phantom could materialize and reach out to touch me. I look up at the surrounding area, sure that the other guards must be close by, which only means they will connect the dots and believe *I* killed this person. Who fucking knows what the Grimaldis will do to me when they realize their lost disgusting daughter stole the life of one of their guards. If they even would care. There's not much those people care about.

I nearly stumble back but will myself to stand my ground as I come face to face with more bodies.

It's a massive bloodbath.

Five guards lie lifeless on the asphalt, their blood seeping through clothes and skin.

Someone massacred all their guards, tearing the flesh from their chests with a knife, leaving behind a mess of terror in its wake.

I gulp the moment I see a piece of paper lying inside one guard's uniform, all drenched in blood and placed near the wound as if to taunt me. I know I should turn away, fucking run as far away from here as possible, and take my bike to the Valenti manor. Alec and Mr. Valenti could help me with this shit, knowing what the fuck to do when the Grimaldi syndicate's guards have been utterly slaughtered. But curiosity gets the better of me, a physical calling that drags and pushes me closer to the note, making me unable to resist it.

With silent, careful steps, I make my way to the guard with trepidation. My stomach ties into knots when the metallic smell of blood worsens, filling my nostrils with the most disgusting smell as I'm forced to lean forward to grab the note. The fucker who left it for me did this on purpose, wanting me to get the guard's blood on my hands.

I grab the note, attempting to avoid the blood, but it's too much. I close my eyes, lips curling in disgust as I see the flesh wound up close. It's enough to make me lose my appetite for days on end.

With bated breath, I bring the note closer, reading the scrawly words written in a now familiar handwriting.

Beautiful, bloodied angel.

Chapter 10
Arcane

UNDER THE HAUNTING GLOW of the moon, I stand with the eerie silence enveloping me, thickening the atmosphere with a palpable apprehension. Secrets hide in the stillness of the night, those that have now been unveiled—for there, all around me, are corpses scattered in the shadows.

I'm holding the note in my hand with such a hard grip; it's a wonder it hasn't yet crumbled into pieces. I should throw it away and allow the wind to carry it far off in the distance, but it's as if I'm stuck in place, my feet glued to the slippery asphalt.

The wind grips my hair, causing it to tangle while I stand motionless, staring out at the dock around me.

Beautiful, bloodied angel.

I read the words over again, not sure if I'm hallucinating or not.

Blood is now on my hands, stained from the paper that must have been left on the corpse not too long ago. I dare take a step closer to the building, passing yet another guard whose chest is ripped open. The metallic tang of blood mingles with the stench of death, assaulting my senses like a heartbroken lover seeking revenge. It's unbearable, causing me to gag as tears rush to the corners of my eyes. Another step away, and I notice yet another note. It's as if they are scattered around, much like the bodies, placed in different areas to make a sort of mystery puzzle for me to solve.

I don't want to, but the gut feeling within me tells me I have to.

I lean forward, grabbing the edge of the note, this one more crumpled than the other. The text is written in what looks like dried blood, red in a darker hue, the handwriting messy and scrawly.

I stare at the words, my brain refusing to comprehend if they even form coherent sentences.

The reaper wants you to find out…who killed the men?

A frown mars my brow, my heart thudding hard beneath my ribcage in an all-too fast rhythm. It makes me slightly dizzy when I glance down to continue reading the other words on the note.

A game to play, my devil.

In an instant, I'm spiraling down memory lane as the notes fall to the ground, their descent unnervingly slow.

"We're going to play a game, you and I. A game that requires you to be observant. Trust no one."

No, no, no, no. I'm shaking my head, staring at the dock with the containers littering the perimeters and the ships by the water. A game, he said, and the next day, he was gone. My lungs start burning, and I barely register that I've started breathing faster as I look at the note once more. It has to be a coincidence.

In that instance, I know it *is* a coincidence. How many criminal organizations haven't had their fair trade of hatred for the Valentis over the years? Even far before I joined them, they had enemies everywhere. All the organizations in this town have, both from within Penumbra Crest and from those around the country.

Rage fills my being, blood boiling like the water left in a kettle for too long until it eventually explodes into bits of pieces, threatening to ruin the world around me. I clench my fists so hard it feels as if my nails will break, pushing into my palms until crescents form.

I look around once more until I can't contain my emotions any longer. "Who's there?" I shout, my voice echoing through the silence of the night. I hear my voice carried away, yet there's no reply, and it pisses me off.

At that moment, I notice movement farther ahead. A subtle shift in the atmosphere and shadows, as if the darkness moves to the side. I squint my eyes but it stills, and I'm not even sure if it was real or all my imagination.

"Get the fuck out of the shadows," I growl, holding the gun in front of me.

I make the stupid decision to stalk forward, refusing to be a little rabbit running away into the hole to hide until the predators are out of their way.

I step beside the bodies scattered around the asphalt, attempting to avoid the blood even if it's everywhere, seeping through the ground and tainting it forever.

"I won't tell you twice. Show your face."

Silence greets me once again, just the sound of the wind as it knocks against the metal of the containers. I stop walking when I reach one, peeking around the corner.

It's empty, and my thoughts scatter like leaves in a storm, tossed around the confines of my brain. Back here, the surroundings are cloaked in obscurity, three containers enveloping the area. Amidst the maze of metal, a small path opens up to my right, leading out onto the other side of the dock.

Slowly, I grab my phone from my pocket, ready to call Alec even if I'm disobeying their commands of not bringing Viper. No way in hell am I bringing that asshole, even if I've never met him. I've heard enough rumors about him and his goddamn family, how they've ruined more people than they've helped. There was even a shady deal between them and the Valentis, though I haven't heard the details of what went down.

I'm just about to press the call button when the oxygen is knocked out of me, my body forcefully pushed against the metal of one of the containers, as if I'm held by an unknown entity.

Both my gun and phone clatter to the ground with a reverberating thud.

I let out a yelp that is quickly silenced by something covering my mouth, preventing me from uttering a single word. My eyes are wide, and my lungs fight for breath.

One moment, I'm alone; the next, I'm confronted by a solid and hard wall preventing me from moving. Confusion clouds my mind as I try to understand what's happening, my brain refusing to cooperate with the rest of my mind. Did a container fall?

Then, I feel it—shudders crawling down my spine like spiders seeking their prey, wanting to scare you off with their too-thin legs running all over you. Disgusting, small insects, horrifying with no point to this world. That's what I feel when something presses against my throat, the moon glinting on the item's surface.

A knife.

There's someone in front of me, holding a goddamn knife to my throat. The blade presses against my skin, threatening to draw blood. My pulse thunders so loud, someone could feel it if they touched my pulse point.

The confusion dissipates as the moon glows, offering some light between the containers and casting shadows on whoever is here with me.

A man, equally as tall, stands before me, broad shoulders held in a posture radiating confidence and something more potent. Like a simmering fire existing underneath the skin, he holds the emotion of anger.

Narrowing my eyes, I feel slightly less brave with a knife against me. I curse myself for dropping the gun, knowing I could have used it as a weapon to protect myself. Now, the darkened figure before me is the one with the advantage.

He presses the knife harder, leaving a stinging sensation, and I know blood must be drawn, a smaller wound forming. His entire form is shrouded in shadows, making me unable to see more of his features.

It feels like minutes in which he merely stands there, drawing precious drops of crimson liquid while not doing anything else. There's a lethal kind of beauty in the dangers around me, and only one question echoes in my mind. If he were the enemy, why isn't he killing me?

Tilting his head as if studying me closely, I finally notice the motorcycle helmet that obscures his face. My soul somersaults within the confines of my bones, losing its grip on me as the realization hits me like an explosion caused by a bomb.

"Do you have any fucking idea of the mess you've created between our families?" he growls out, voice laced with an anger that can't be tamed.

For a second, I'm stunned to silence, unable to make sense of any of this. The next, I'm looking into his eyes—or at least what I think are his eyes through the visor of the helmet—sneering at him.

A mistake, I realize, when he applies more pressure with the knife, widening my eyes with the chilling fear that he's *actually going to cut me.*

He drives me back against the container, my skull colliding with the surface as it elicits a throbbing ache. The tilt of his head, more aggressive now, underscores the depth of his rage, his next words dripping with seething animosity. "Do you?"

I decide not to reply, frankly unable to with how tight he grips me. I fear that if I utter a word, the blade will cut deeper than it already has, and it's a risk I can't take.

As if noticing my train of thought, he slowly removes the knife, but his hand remains just as steady on me, preventing me from going anywhere.

"You were supposed to bring me with you, *Arcane*." He spits out my name as if it's a curse, leaving a disgusting aftertaste on his tongue that he needs to get rid of.

Within a moment of resolution, I will my muscles to loosen, using my arm to wrench free from his grip and throw an uppercut, leaving him stumbling back from shock. It gives me the escape I need to slip out of my confinement, using my foot to kick away my gun so he won't reach it.

"You're Viper, huh?" I pronounce his name with as much hatred as I can muster, letting my words pour out with a tone laced with disgust, much more potent than his. I take a step back right when he takes one forward, showing how pathetic I am, and I scold myself. "Tell your boss I have no intention of working with you," I spit out.

Yet again, that tilt of his head betrays emotions I can't

decipher. I'm left grappling with the mystery of his expression and cannot discern his facial features or any clues to his identity beneath the helmet. All are covered by a single helmet, hiding him from the world. Somehow, I'm still sure he's *the* Viper. One of the most notorious bikers in the whole Penumbra Crest.

"I'm my own boss." There's a scoff in his voice as he says this, and though I can't see his eyes, I know they're staring right at me.

His sheer presence is overwhelming, taking over the eerie space around us until it becomes one sole thing—him.

Never once do I break my gaze from him, keeping track of all his movements. I swallow harshly when he steps closer, and I attempt to appear unbothered, but it's hard when I know he's the one with the weapon now. He has his knife, whereas I dropped my gun.

His knife is covered with blood glistening off the sharp blade in the gentle, silvery glow of the moon.

Blood.

"You—" I take a shuddering breath, attempting to control both the fright and the irritation filling every nerve ending within me. "You killed those guards." It sounds more like a question than a statement.

I imagine him smirking underneath the helmet, finding amusement in my confusion and rage. He remains silent, anger palpable in the tense stillness that hangs between us, allowing the wind to breeze against the unyielding metal surfaces of the containers.

"You fucking killed those guards."

Rage is a potent thing visible in me, yet it's also one of the most dangerous emotions you can show to your enemy. Staying calm and composed at all times serves as an advantage when you're in checkmate mode. That allows you to keep your mind in control. Whereas rage takes over everything you're feeling until the only thing you sense is just that. I'm fuming, my hands shaking with uncontrolled emotions.

If Mr. Valenti saw me right now, he'd throw me to the wolves, our sworn enemies, or worse—condemn me to the isolation chamber hidden in their basement. It's a room meant for those associates, or even made men, who dare betray the syndicate. A shudder skates over my skin as I think about it, forgetting the existence of the biker for a moment.

"So what?" His voice barely cuts through the howling wind.

Grounding myself, I take yet another step back, telling myself it's because I don't want him near me. But I'd be lying if I said that was the *only* reason.

He draws closer, and with another container behind me, I'm unable to put more distance between us.

"So what?" he repeats, sending goosebumps erupting across my arms.

I think about all the reasons why I'm annoyed. The fact that the Grimaldis would know someone was here, disposing of their guards with no remorse. It will make them suspicious, heightening their security and making it more intact without any way to slip through their defenses.

"If you're so adamant on this mission, *Viper*, then you should know the *so what*," I say as calmly as I can. "Fucking idiot."

In an instant, I'm slammed against the container with such ferocity that my head collides sharply against the metal, sending waves of dizziness to swim up the surface. The world blurs into a hazy picture for a moment.

All I feel is the lack of air as he encircles his hand around my throat, not enough to kill me, but enough to weaken me. He's tantalizingly close, the heat from his body brushing against mine and creating a different, *forbidden*, tension full of desire and danger.

His hand is right on my pulse point, trapping me in his hold, and I realize fighting is useless. Predators always chase the prey that fight or resist.

A silent and unmoving bunny is a living bunny.

Despite the fear gripping me, there's a certain thrill in our proximity, as if I'm chasing the danger by desiring to stand close to him.

He increases the pressure until my chin involuntarily tilts upward, forcing me to meet his gaze. Tingling sensations cascade through my body in this twisted moment, having always enjoyed the arousing brink between life and death, no matter how perverse.

Underneath the tinted visor, the shadows of his eyes loom, darker and more intense than mine. They bore into me with a seething rage and hatred, yet there's something else I can't name.

This is a man who kills ruthlessly, enough to earn a reputation as a notorious biker. The second-born son of the García cartel, whereas I'm only a made woman in the underground world of Penumbra Crest.

The way he grips my throat, pressing his thumb against the pulse that could render me unconscious if pressed hard enough, reminds me too much of a person I'd rather forget. Someone who doesn't deserve a place in my thoughts. It makes my heart ache in ways I never wished for, and I push those memories away, locking them in a box far down in my subconscious that it will take years to dig out.

"Here's how things are gonna go, little angel." He sneers the awful nickname like an insult, a cold glint in his eyes. "I possess knowledge that neither you nor anyone in your family are privy to, and I also have the schematics." A smirk tugs at his lips, and I dig my nails into my palm.

So, he stole the damn schematics, proving the fact he killed that person in the warehouse.

I interrupt him before he can elaborate. "Are you so attached to your knife that you can't help but hold it close to your chest?" I flutter my eyelids, cursing my stupid mouth for uttering a comment like that. Well, too late now, fucker.

He stands so close that I feel the subtle rise and fall of his chest with every breath, each one deeper than the last—filled with irritation from my comment. *Bingo.*

"Don't you ever fucking interrupt me again," he growls,

the knife grazing my skin, drawing forth a drop of blood, yet not enough to cut too deeply. "You're going to gather your thoughts and start cooperating," he continues with a tone full of malice. There's something so radiant and potent about him; it's overwhelming, like being scorched by a hot iron. "Or else, there will be a war between our families. And trust me, you don't want that."

"You have no idea what I want," I sneer.

He scoffs. "Oh, but I do. I hold the power to put you down like a sick dog in need of saving, or like a ship swallowed by the largest wave, meeting its dooming destiny. You don't want to be that ship crashing into the waves."

In the blink of an eye, he vanishes, leaving me alone amidst the corpses of the guards and the macabre notes he undoubtedly left behind.

He fades away as if he was never here to begin with. But the echoes of his presence linger, leaving behind a metaphor of words crashing against my insides like the deadliest virus.

Chapter 11
Arcane

"HOW'S THE MISSION GOING?" Mr. Valenti's words cut through the tense atmosphere of the conference room, where I sit hidden in the shadows, eavesdropping on the meeting unfolding.

One I should be attending, yet one I didn't even know was happening until I saw the Garcías enter the perimeters of our manor.

Since the Valentis are working with the Garcías, Antonio called a meeting between the two families to discuss important business matters. It's the first-ever official meeting between them in a conference room, with everyone attending.

Everyone except me.

It infuriates me to my core, forcing me to clench my fists from the overwhelming emotions raging within me, or else I'd do something stupid like punch the locker I'm hiding inside. A plant right outside covers some of my view, but I only need to listen.

I didn't think they'd discuss these matters, but *of fucking course,* the criminal families in this world don't call in for meetings without reason. The skin breaks underneath my fingertips with the force with which the anger radiates through my body. It's a smoldering one that brews underneath my calm exterior.

"It's going great," a darkened voice erupts in the room.

As usual, he hasn't taken off his helmet, face obscured by it, and veils his identity from prying eyes. It makes me wonder if I'll ever get to see the face behind the mask.

Why do I even care?

Mr. Valenti arches an eyebrow at Viper when he steps forward, obviously not believing him. Has Alec betrayed me? Divulged to his father that I've failed to cooperate with Viper on our missions?

The mere thought causes a heavy feeling to settle in my gut, its weight dragging me down as my muscles tense involuntarily. I feel like a helpless rabbit caught in a cage while waiting for any of the wolves to realize I'm here. Out in the world, I'm thriving, being the she-wolf, but I stand no chance against a room filled with two of the most dangerous criminal families in this town.

"Has it now?" Mr. Valenti voices his thoughts, a look of distrust in his eyes. "Because it has come to my attention by my associates that you and Ms. Grimaldi haven't collaborated on these preparations."

I grit my teeth until the muscles in my cheeks spasm from the pain at the mention of my former surname, causing hatred to erupt within me. He fucking gave me the Valenti name to protect me. I've been with them for the other half of my life, fighting my ass off to prove myself and my worth. *Wasn't that enough?*

I close my eyes, steeling myself for the explosion to erupt when Viper reveals he hasn't worked with me at all—mainly because I've been keeping him out of this. Do I regret it? Fuck no.

A strange stiffness momentarily grips Viper's posture at the mention of the Grimaldi name, but it quickly dissipates, and he relaxes. He sighs, facing Mr. Valenti head-on, with the rest of the Garcías positioned behind him. The room bristles with tension with everyone on high alert, surrounded by security guards.

Seeing Viper here and not his father raises questions within me about a possible leadership shift, making me wonder what I missed regarding the García cartel.

"That person must have the wrong information because we've been working *very* closely."

It's not just his composed demeanor that gives away his nonchalance; it's the unhurried shift of his weight from one foot to the other, as if lying to another mafia boss is nothing to be bothered about.

"Do you have any proof of this?" Mr. Valenti asks after one minute of thick silence.

"On June twenty-eight, at midnight, was the time for the congregation between the Grimaldis at the Ivanovas," he reveals, voice unwavering, like a solid wall of confidence. "You wanted me as a business partner, and here's my deal. Both families are working together, and the proof is in this hard drive. It contains written documented plans, complete with time stamps, discussing the forthcoming delivery scheduled in five days."

He allows his words to hang heavy in the air as if we've all been sucked underneath a suffocating blanket. Mr. Valenti's hand twitches, the only indication of his distress and a sign that this is the first time he's heard about this. No one knew about the Ivanovas—another of the five ruling families in Penumbra Crest— conspiring with the Grimaldis, and no one knew they had moved up the date for the car to be delivered to their dock.

Viper holds up the drive, but right as Mr. Valenti tries to snatch it out of his hand, Viper throws it toward another male behind him. The resemblance between the other man and Viper's father, Louis García, is uncanny, with the same shape of nose and eyes. They must be siblings.

"I'd like a personal meeting with Arcane to go over the information within this drive."

My pulse beats harder at the way he pronounces my name, his voice so dark and masculine, with an alluring tone that could trap anyone.

"Speaking of which, why isn't Arcane here?" He looks around the room, tilting his head as he stares at Mr. Valenti, who clenches his fist at the obvious disrespect.

"That's none of your business. This is a meeting for us men," he seethes through his teeth.

Viper tilts his head. "And yet, you allow a woman to take over a heist as important as this."

There's something about his words that doesn't appear misogynist at all, and it fills me with a sensation I cannot quite make out.

"Don't question me." Mr. Valenti's voice is deadly cold as he speaks, causing the rest of the Garcías to glance at each other.

"I'll make it clear for you, Benjamin Valenti." Viper's voice carries a sharp edge. "When I ask for something, I shall receive it. I expect Arcane to meet me by the docks tonight, and then she can share the details of this hard drive with you. If she refuses or fails to comply, this information will stay buried, and we'll have the upper hand."

My breath hitches at the silent threat in his words. How the fuck did he come across those files?

Of course. He stole the schematics before I had the chance. *Dammit!* I'd been searching for those a while ago, to get my hands on their detailed plans and logistics for their delivery with the seller of the car that has the drive, but Viper had beat me to it.

The meeting soon dies out as both families turn to leave the conference with a formal goodbye. I wait for a few seconds, making sure no one is inside the room before I slip out of the locker. The cramped space has left my body aching from the uncomfortable position in which I sat.

Opening the locker, ready to get out of there and think of my plan on how to proceed next, I'm suddenly met by a hard, solid wall where I should be able to roam freely.

Shock renders me motionless as I stop in my tracks, looking up through thick eyelashes. It's not a concrete wall; it's a wall of muscles, defined underneath a dark shirt. My heart is a frantic bird attempting to escape my chest as I meet shadowed eyes behind the tinted helmet. Despite the obscured features, it's as if his intense gaze pierces through.

"Tsk, tsk. Little angel, spying on a conference she wasn't invited to," Viper remarks with a tinge of disapproval and amusement, crossing his arms over his chest which accentuates the bulging muscles beneath. *And those damned veins.* The sight of his tattoos adorning his arms like sleeves is undeniably captivating, and I feel myself staring at only them for a brief moment.

He's the same height as me, but with me crouching down, he towers above me. A swift breeze of his scent washes over my senses and trails to my nostrils, something leather-like mixed with an earthy cologne. I swallow hard, trying to fend off the effect of his closeness. Despite my efforts, his gaze feels directed at me, as if I'm the sole focus of his attention, hating every second of it.

"Get out of my way," I say when I notice he's blocking my escape from the locker.

I remain crouched, muscles straining from the position. All he does is look at me, amusement littering his features. It's in the subtle tilt of his head, the way his posture exudes a relaxed confidence. He doesn't move out of the way.

"Get the fuck out of my way," I growl, trying to push past him. It doesn't work at first, but then he finally lets me go, and I'm out of the locker.

Yet the moment I'm ready to get out of there, he traps me between the wall and his body, standing like a lethal force before me. His scent is more prominent now and seeks its way into my soul. How he stares at me causes flutters in my stomach, creatures with sharp wings whose sole mission is to slice me dry, leaving me to die alone in my misery without any mercy.

I'm ready for him to strike me for disobeying the rules and codex of our criminal world. *Don't ever spy on a meeting.* Anyone else who'd been in my position would have been executed immediately. Doesn't he have the stomach to do it? I've seen and heard how ruthlessly he kills people; he's unforgiving in his ways.

"What are you doing here, little devil?"

I'm trapped in his presence, a spell bewitching me in place and rendering me helpless against this criminal man in front of me. Why didn't I carry a gun when I decided to spy on this meeting? A weapon would've given me leverage, a means to force him out of my way.

Feeling daring, I reach out to remove his helmet, and to my surprise, he doesn't stop me. As my fingers brush against the surface, my heart quickens its pace in anticipation. But it's short-lived as I discover the balaclava mask underneath, concealing everything except his deep brown eyes and lips.

He smirks at me, before stroking my cheek, eyes remaining

unwavering with a relentless intensity. As I move my head away, his hand follows, grazing against my skin even when I don't want it to.

His upper body presses against mine, and I feel the brush of his leg. A moment of silence passes as his thumb delicately traces my lip as if savoring every tingling sensation. I'm locked in a trance, rendered speechless and unable to utter a word, as if I'm an outsider from another planet.

His thumb continues its gentle exploration of my lip, and before my brain can understand anything, his leg nudges my own in a subtle move.

Shock fills every feature as my eyes widen, struggling to grasp what's going on.

"What are you doing?" I blurt out, my voice tinged with disbelief and apprehension.

He doesn't say anything, merely continuing to graze my lips, as if his movements enthrall me. My pulse beats fiercely, the rush of blood drowning out any other sound. But amidst the pounding in my ears, I hear the change in his breath as it becomes heavier, huskier somehow.

"What the fuck are you doing?" I repeat, trying to shift away from him.

All of a sudden, his lips meet mine, and I realize it's one meant to devour, slaughter, and annihilate, never to be tender or caring. He connects with me in a bruising kiss, his teeth grazing my lips until he sinks them down, biting. I feel the tang of metallic, knowing he bit down, drawing blood.

I'm too shocked to do anything, too captivated by the enchanting kiss to comprehend the turn of events. I barely know him, and yet I allowed him to kiss me. The realization sends a jolt of confusion and apprehension through me, but I'm powerless to resist the allure of his embrace.

The rivaling family's second-born son.

The Viper García.

When I try to push him away, he only kisses me harder as his hand finds my neck, anchoring me in place. His thigh presses against my clit above the skirt, igniting a wave of pleasure that makes me lose myself as I forget about my surroundings. Pure pleasure washes over me in ways I never wished for, a primal hunger within that begs to be touched and devoured, as the depraved piece of my soul has wanted. Though I resist returning his kiss, when he bites down on my lips again and leaves a stinging sensation, I'm compelled to surrender my soul to the devil before me for the taking.

Moving his thigh, he rubs against my throbbing clit, almost causing my eyes to roll back, but I quickly recover. For a second, I swear I feel him smirk against my lips, but I dare not open my eyes, afraid that this daydream will end.

Without a second thought, too lost in myself, I find myself recklessly grinding against him while seeking that tiny piece of pleasure I haven't felt for years. A subtle—ever so silent—hiss of breath escapes me, which only spurs him on.

His hand spans my stomach, slowly moving downward teasingly slow, as though committing me to memory. Then, his hand lifts my skirt, sliding my panties to the side before his cold fingers touch my aching clit once more, igniting a fire in me.

As his fingers breach my entrance, each deliberate thrust brings me to the edge of pleasure. It takes everything in me not to fall over from how my legs are trembling, leaning against the wall as if it were a lifeline. I cling to a semblance of strength, refusing to allow everything I'm feeling to show in my expression.

This is utterly fucked, but I can't seem to get away.

"You like this, don't you?" he breathes against my ear. "Your body betrays you. You're going to come now like the little devil you are. Come for me."

His last word is a growl, and before I know it, I'm coating his fingers with wetness, making them slick as I come undone, surrendering to the intoxicating sensations taking over my body. My limbs are trembling in the aftermath, the act causing me to pant heavily as I try to catch my breath.

As the haze of desire begins to lift, shock brings me back to reality. The fantasy I was momentarily lost in shatters, replaced by a torrent of anger radiating deep within.

My heart plummets to the pit of my stomach, and without a moment's hesitation, I push him away with all my strength. Taken aback by the force of my action, he staggers back. The palpable intensity of my fury fills the air, evident like fuming waves.

"What the fuck was that?" I shout.

At this moment, I don't care about the risk of anyone overhearing me. All I care about is confronting him, challenging his audacity for thinking he has the right to come into my fucking territory and do things like that.

The first intimate moment I've ever shared with someone since him.

The realization of it claws at my chest, making me want to tear out my chest because of it. My heart feels like a broken mirror within my chest, without any chance of saving.

Viper merely smirks in response, backing off with a promising glint in his eyes—a promise of retribution and something more sinister yet to come.

Despite the uneasy feeling gnawing at me, I can't figure out what he's up to. But I know that whatever it is, it's deemed to be foreboding.

Chapter 12
Arcane

THE SILENCE OF THE night wraps around me like a shroud as I leave my bike a few blocks away from the docks, deciding to walk the rest of the distance. With a gun safely tucked into my back pocket, easily accessible if the need arises, I tread cautiously, moving as quietly as the world around me.

It's one of those nights where the silence in my head is louder than any thoughts, screaming out their void and impeccably doubting feelings that disturb the peace. For years, I haven't had anyone who could understand me. Once, there was one, but he didn't stay by my side. He was a liar and a thief, stealing my heart and leaving me incapable of loving anyone else. Oh, if only he understood how hard it is to breathe when the air is too thin around me.

Beautiful crime, I think as I traverse the empty streets, memories flood my mind unwantedly. He committed a beautiful, tragic crime when he left me to fight alone in a world where women are too often regarded as disposable pawns in men's games of power and dominance.

Will things ever change? Is the world condemned to be a place where one gender holds dominion? It's a realm tarnished by judgmental stares, where women face prejudice simply for their gender, and men dismiss them for merely existing.

My feet pound against the asphalt of the sidewalk, a burner phone pressed to my ear with Alec's voice crackling through the other line.

"Father announced that Viper wants to meet you by the docks to discuss a drive he found," Alec says, voice betraying a hint of tension. He's choosing his words carefully, lying to me as if I didn't already know that Viper told him that during yesterday's conference meeting.

Suppressing the urge to confront him about it, I reply. "Got it. I'll be there soon."

"Good, we need to extract as much information as possible. Use whatever tactics necessary to coax it out of him if he doesn't voluntarily reveal anything of importance. We need to get to the drive before he does and destroy it."

His words only mean one thing—the Valentis don't fully trust the García family like I initially thought. They're only using them for valuable intel. Relief washes over me. I never liked them, anyway.

"Don't worry, Alec. I got this under control, trust me," I tell him, ready to end the call before remembering a question that's been brewing in my mind ever since yesterday. "By the way, what happened to Louis García? Why isn't he the one leading the communication?"

I've pondered that question ever since I saw Viper taking the boss's position yesterday.

"Didn't you hear? He was killed in a gang war between the Ivanovas and the Garcías, forcing Viper to take over."

As Alec's words sink in, they send an unexpected wave of shock over me. I never knew Viper had taken over the former leader of the García cartel, a stark reminder of the world we inhabit, where we can lose those we hold dear anytime.

Then, Alec ends the call with a few words of encouragement.

I count my steps toward the dock, pushing away the nerves that threaten to derail me. There's no place for nerves when I'm supposed to meet the notorious biker—now apparently the leader—of the García cartel.

Arriving at the docks, I scan my surroundings. The absence of guards makes suspicion rise within me, sending off alarm bells in my mind. I wonder if the Grimaldis have found out about their killed guards, and whether they know who committed such a heinous crime. I swallow what feels like molten lava at the thought of it, hating my underlying apprehension toward that family.

The only sound audible is the symphony of waves crashing against the dock farther away; despite that, a sense of foreboding chills me to my bones.

I stand utterly still, assessing my surroundings closely, when the creaking sound of a branch to my right breaks the silence of the eerie atmosphere. My head whips that way, the sound piercing through the air.

Another beat of silence passes when a second sound comes from behind me. With lightning speed, my eyes dart around my dimly lit surroundings for any sign of movement, slowly retrieving the gun from my pocket.

I dare not take a breath as I wait for whoever is around me to step out of the shadows and reveal themselves. It feels like I'm standing there for hours, nothing happening, making me feel as if I've been tricked. An utter fool for falling for the trick of someone being here; it's probably my imagination running wild.

I move from my position, feeling the oppressive silence enveloping me like a thick blanket, suffocating the oxygen from a raging fire. A sensation I'm well too aware of seeps into my marrow and chills my bones like icy fingers gripping me, threatening to drag my body under the earth. Unlike the exhilarating thrill of danger that I've felt before—moments when the eyes watching me feel more territorial than predatory, more intense than terrifying—this one feels different. It's as if this is more ominous, tinged with a sense of foreboding that makes my subconscious scream at me to instantly leave.

My heart is a steadfast drumbeat of unease as I step forward, ignoring the warning alarms that heighten the sense of unseen eyes scrutinizing my every move.

A thunderous bang erupts ahead, wrenching my soul from the confines of my bones.

Nothing is there.

With hesitant steps, I move toward where I heard the sound, wondering what the fuck that was. I curse my curiosity for leading me to a place that might as well be my downfall, but it's too late now. With stiff shoulders, I peek around the corner, only noticing a speaker on the ground hidden between two containers.

Another sound crackles through the air, and I clench my fist in frustration.

"Motherfucker," I curse under my breath, feeling a mix of stupidity and annoyance at whatever twisted game he's playing.

Thereafter, silence ensues until a tape starts playing. My brow furrows when a voice begins speaking, and I recognize the darker tones and low timbres. It's dark, slithering its way into my soul with a gentle yet harsh caress, and the image of him pushing me against the wall the day before displays in my mind, causing my cheeks to heat.

"Here you are, little angel. As you can see, I'm not here now, am I?" A chuckle erupts, making my nipples pebble underneath my hoodie. *"One mile from here, there's a cliffside where the cliffs meet the water in endless waves. A beautifully tragic place, might I say. Meet me there, and we will discuss the information on the hard drive. Ruin any evidence of this speaker*

when you're done listening. We cannot have any trace of the organizations knowing about this."

Confusion swirls within my mind as I stare at the device, pondering the meaning of his words. He told me to meet him here by the docks, revealing the location in front of both of our families. Now, he changes his mind, telling me to meet him at some other place. Is this a joke? Or is he truly that paranoid of anyone overhearing our conversation?

The questions make suspicion rise within me, uncertainty a gnawing feeling, and I'm torn between the choices of what I should do.

Clutching the radio tightly, I bring it with me as I navigate the desolate streets again, climbing onto my bike. The image of the location where he wants to meet haunts my mind, a heartbreaking reminder of those damned cliffs. It's a sacred place Viper's now withholding, staining it with his intense presence and lurking shadow.

No. I make my decision. I won't go there.

Instead, I rev the engine of my Kawasaki, speeding off onto the winding roads that lead the path home. I will not let him dictate what I should do; it's his fucking fault for not telling me the right meeting place immediately.

It takes shorter than usual to drive my way home. Everyone in the neighborhood is asleep as I park my bike outside my apartment.

When I reach my door, an invisible hand seems to squeeze

the life from my heart, leaving a sudden emptiness as it spreads a hollow feeling. It sucks the warmth from within as I stare at the sight before me.

A note.

An ominous fucking note, its presence changing everything I thought I knew.

He knows where I live. The realization hits me like a sledgehammer, making me stumble backward before regaining my composure.

Of course, deep down, I'd suspected he was the one slicing my shoulder weeks ago, invading my home. I reread the chilling message, each word searing into my mind like a brand, yet they barely make sense through the cloud of shock.

Shock soon gives way to a fierce rage that bubbles up inside me, boiling over with a ferocity I cannot contain. He dare fucking come to my apartment and threaten me? *That self-observed fucking asshole.*

Without a second to spare, I tear the note from my door, fingers curling into fists as I enter the apartment. The air crackles with a sense of unease as I methodically activate the security alarm, which will alert me if anyone tries to break in. I double-check every lock and window, ensuring no one can trespass. I make sure he hasn't entered my apartment while I was gone before finally retreating to the safety of my bedroom.

Adrenaline shoots through me as if I've been drugged with the strongest chemical before I grab the gun in my hand, the weight of it a comforting reassurance.

Minutes drag on with agonizing slowness as I steel myself for the inevitable to come, not knowing what the future holds.

Chapter 13
Who Am I?
I guess you'll soon find out

THEY SAY SCARS ON the body fade with time, their jagged edges softening, their raised skin smoothening, and the once violent pink hues mellowing into nothingness. As years pass, these scars will gradually diminish until they're barely noticed. I wonder whether this is because we grow accustomed to their presence or if they truly fade into oblivion.

Yet, what about the invisible scars? The ones that don't mark the skin's surface? Those etch onto the fabric of our souls, an imprint we will never be rid of.

They say scars on your body eventually heal, while the scars on our souls never do. It's a true testament to my body, the scars staining me like a brand I cannot rid myself of.

Empathy and sympathy are foreign concepts to me, emotions I could never grasp. While I know I'm meant to harbor some form of emotion toward others, be it remorse or regret, that simply isn't me.

I kill without feeling anything, it's why they call me notorious. Sometimes, I take a life as an experiment, if only to see if I'm capable of feeling. Each time, I end up disappointed—or at least, I think it's disappointment, like a vague ache in my chest. My emotions are few and far between, as they've always been.

Growing up as I did, I suppose it was an advantage not to feel pain, betrayal, or hurt. In the criminal world, weakness is a luxury one cannot afford—only a stoic façade that unnerves the enemies.

Most children would have been traumatized by what I endured. The worst of it was when my father, in a twisted attempt to teach me a lesson, shot my shoulder when I was but a fifteen-year-old boy. He claimed it was to test my ability to stitch my wounds without shedding a tear like a "shitty baby." My right hand wears the scars from when he forced me to grasp scalding flames—to test my endurance, he'd said.

That moment particularly affected me, and I've been forced to wear a leather glove to cover it up. Kids like to fucking stare at things they shouldn't.

Other times, he'd say he loved me if only to gain my trust again. All to mold me into the heir he wanted, but I never intended to be that person for the Grimaldi syndicate.

Until one rainy day changed everything.

I still feel the chill of that moment when masked figures emerged from the shadows, ambushing me and holding me at gunpoint. I realized they knew everything about me, details I'd never divulged to anyone.

My memories before the orphanage are fragmented, but the stern-faced man in the photographs at my dead mother's apartment remains in my mind. I recall her tears as she used to gaze upon those images, whispering wishes for a different life untainted by darkness when she thought I was asleep in my room.

My mother had fled from my biological father, determined to shield me from the criminal world that had tormented her. Yet, despite her efforts, fate had a way of being cruel.

Fourteen years after her passing, that same man from the photographs resurfaced, threatening to take everything from me if I didn't comply. They demanded I start anew as the heir to their criminal family because the firstborn son had died—a brother whom my mother had left behind when he refused to escape with us. When they ambushed me, they thought I had something to lose, and I scoffed at them because I had nothing.

Until they showed a photograph of *her* sleeping in bed with her shirt riddled up against her stomach, taken from the point where I used to sneak into her room during the nights.

They threatened to kill the only person I've ever been capable of feeling something for.

I did as they said, no matter how much it hurt to leave her—I couldn't let any danger befall her. For years, I bided my time at the

García cartel, waiting for the moment my father would die. When he died in a gang war, I finally got the free reins to fully take over as the second-born son, evidently earning my freedom and respect from my cousins and associates.

He was the biological father I never got the chance to meet before the orphanage—Louis García—the absent father my mother had tried to hide me from before she passed away when I was nine.

It seemed she was a García, and so was I.

IT'S TIME, I THINK as I slip into the shadows slithering around the building before me.

The moment I've been waiting for during all those agonizing years of solitude, forced to do my duty as the heir to the García cartel even when I didn't want to.

It was a long time ago when I was ripped from the sanctuary I once knew and thrust into the world of being an heir to one of the infamous families in Penumbra Crest. Years since I had to fabricate my death and betrayed the only person I've ever cared about, all to protect her.

As the years have passed, my indifference has grown, and now I no longer care about it all. It's become a duty as much as it's become a part of the game I've been playing with myself—a twisted game full of lies and deceit, with people suffering underneath my thumb.

My beautiful little angel. At last mine for the taking, like an inevitable doom that no one could've predicted. Certainly not my so-called family.

My father would roll around in his grave if he found out I'm this reckless, going on missions that shouldn't involve me but making them my responsibility anyway. He'd call me pussy-whipped, just because he's never felt the tingling obsession in his fingertips, like a craving and need that urges you to purge what's yours.

A don to an infamous criminal family should strictly act on business-related things, but all that's ever been on my mind for the past few years is *her.*

Arcane.

Every step she makes, every room she breathes in, every person she speaks to. I've made it my business to know all about her ever since I infiltrated her home years ago, needing to know every single thing she did. She might exceed me on other things, but she'll never beat me when it comes to hacking, no matter how good she thinks she is.

If she's that good, how come I've been watching over her for so long without her knowledge?

How come she doesn't know to search the room for any bugged cameras?

I've been watching very closely, keeping track of everything she does to make sure she is ready. And here she is. Unprepared for me, yet ready all the same.

She'll beg for me by the time I'm done. She'll wish she never met me, but it's a bit too late now. She should have thought about that the moment she gave up on me. Not that I would blame her. I'd give up on me, too.

But I never gave up on her.

My beautiful, little devil angel.

Breathing in the fresh air of the forest around me, I know it will be even more crisp once I get my hands on her. I've been biding my time all these years, silently waiting in the shadows for the right opportunity to finally break free from the holds keeping me captured.

She's been my sanctuary, my only train of thought.

They tried to take her away from me, the fucking Valentis, but I won't let them. I might step out of line as the current don of the organization and start another gang war, but I frankly can't care. She's been my sole purpose, my only darling one for as long as I can remember, and I'm not about to give her up.

Ever since Louis García—my father—passed away in a gang war a few months ago, I've been slowly taking over the organization, handling the business and drugs along with the rest of my family. I'm the head of the heist we're preparing for, with my little devil intentionally keeping me out of it. She's too goddamn stubborn for her own self.

Unfortunately for her, I've been shadowing her every move, privy to the intel she lacks. That's why I arranged for our meeting at the cliffside. I knew she wouldn't agree, which is why I'm concealed within the forest near her home, biding my time for the right moment while deactivating her security alarm.

She once told me I could do to her whatever I wished, and, well, I assume it still applies now. A smirk dances upon my lips as I examine the zip ties in my grasp and the chloroform tucked in my pocket, thinking over my plan. It's been torturous staying away for this long, but I've honed the art of discretion.

Observing her in all her glory has only fueled my obsession, making me want to plunge deep inside her to take what I haven't felt for an eternity—what's rightfully mine. Now, it's finally time.

I'm coming for you, my little devil. There's no salvation from the reaper that will purge your soul.

Chapter 14
Arcane

A TANGIBLE FEAR COILS down my spine like a hungry beast. I can't do anything to fight the paralysis keeping me immobile. There's no saving grace, only the haunting presence lurking somewhere inside my room.

I try to breathe steadier, seeking refuge in the rhythm of my heartbeat, yet it proves futile. Especially as I sense someone drawing nearer in the darkness blanketing the room.

It's as if I'm hurtling over the edge of a deadly cliff, chasing the end of the world with the speed at which I descend. I cannot tell whether I'm awake or not. A twisting figure appears, hovering above me with an aura of danger, a mask obscuring its features.

"I'm sorry, devangel. I never wanted to wake you."

The words are a chilling brush against my skin, frosty tendrils reaching out to devour me. My heart pounds hard in my ribcage, and I struggle against the paralysis that binds me. Even in my confusion, I want to believe this is a state of limbo where reality blurs with nightmares. Though I know better.

That voice is all too familiar, *achingly* so, piercing through flesh and bone like a sword. It's not merely the voice that renders me motionless, it's that goddamn nickname. It's unsettling, dredging up memories I would rather bury, of *him* calling me devil and angel, combining the two and coining the nickname 'devangel.' Yet, my mind stubbornly refuses to understand who it's coming from.

That voice shouldn't know that nickname. It doesn't make sense.

All oxygen is gone from my lungs. No matter how hard I try, I can't seem to wake up from this torment.

The crashing of waves against rocks, violent with no source of remorse or mercy, is a reminder of reality. With mounting dread, I strain to break free from the grip that holds me captive in a vortex of hell.

I manage to open my eyes and am met with the sight of the figure hovering above me. With a surge of dread, I jolt upright when the paralysis releases its hold on me.

My relief is short-lived when I realize I'm bound, hands tied above my head, restrained by what feels like a silken band. The figure before me remains silent, their breath the only sound in the room—a gentle rhythm with an enigmatic weight, as if they're in agony.

A gentle touch trails along my thigh, inching closer to where the fabric of my sleeping shorts ends. My heart races as I remain bound, offered like a lamb to the gods above, awaiting a sacrifice for justice to unfold. A finger draws near my most intimate area, sending electric pulses of anticipation through me that make my breath hitch.

Incoherent words escape my lips as another touch grazes my cheek, tender yet unsettling, as if I'm something precious. A lover's touch. The other hand slips underneath my sleeping shorts, igniting a fiery passion even as I try to resist.

My eyes adjust to the darkness, and the masked man becomes clearer, causing my blood to run cold like a bucket of ice.

"Shh, go back to sleep." The voice is soothing, rocking me back to an endless sleep that wants to drag me down.

Viper.

He's here, he came for me. His name echoes in my mind, a chilling reminder of how I disobeyed his command. My mind screams at me to get away as fast as possible, tendrils of fear slithering down the pit of my stomach. The other part of me—my body—yearns for his touch and craves the forbidden pleasure he offers. Wasn't this what I wanted before when he fingered me inside the conference room? All the longing, raging gazes between us would eventually lead us down this path.

But where the fuck am I?

No matter how much I squirm, his hand stays firmly on my cheek while the other trails to my clit, applying gentle pressure. In the dim light, his eyes seem to darken, like two slits of shadows, watching me unravel beneath his touch.

Something penetrates me, bringing out pleasure like no other as I'm torn between intoxication and the nagging sense of unease. I fight against the invisible leash ensnaring me, but it's pointless.

Drifting in and out of consciousness, it feels as though I'm tumbling over that cliff once more. My eyes spring open, my stomach and clit pulsating with conflicting desires. Instead of falling, I'm soaring toward the clouds, only to plummet when waves of immense pleasure overtake everything. Gasping for breath, I realize my mouth is pressed against a pillow, my body convulsing in euphoria. Every instinct rebels against it, yet an undeniable pull draws me toward the forbidden euphoria coursing through me. Fingers plunge inside me, finding that sweet spot with precision.

Lost in the maze of my mind, a moan betrays me as those skilled fingers curl. I try to form words, to beg him to stop, but everything is too much. In my half-conscious mind, his fingers slip deeper, plunging into me over and over. I'm engulfed in an overwhelming ecstasy, sending me into a sublime bliss.

Unwanted moans mingle with fear, intensifying the sensation. Before I know it, I'm grinding my hips against his fingers, riding the crest of pleasure. With each tantalizing caress, he coaxes forth sensations of arousal, and I crave more of his sinful touch.

A deep, growl-like chuckle emanates from him, forcing me back into reality, but his fingers are still inside of me, and I'm teetering on the edge of surrender. With each added finger, the ecstasy consumes me completely. I try to stifle my moans, but his hand slides to my throat, squeezing. Eventually, I'm forced to release those moans wanting to tear from my throat, almost drowning out the relentless sounds of the waves outside.

He brings me to another orgasm—unyielding to the irresistible sensations overwhelming me, letting him feel me as I come undone.

I'm in a dizzy haze of not comprehending anything, ensnared in a web of desire and uncertainty as the realization crashes over me.

I just came from being fingered, all while half awake.

As I begin to wake from the surreal dream, I expect to find myself in the comfort of my bed. Yet, the sight before me is unfamiliar—a window revealing clouds outside, dark and raging with the threat of an oncoming storm.

I'm not at home.

The gentle touch against my face continues, a touch so tender it makes my heart slow down its pace as if recognizing the move, yet it's not the contact of skin that meets mine. It's a leather glove assaulting my senses.

"Where I am?" I mumble incoherently.

No reply. One hand glides against my thigh again, causing goosebumps to spread over my body. I can't remember much, but I remember falling asleep in my bedroom, with only silence soothing my screaming mind.

Where the hell am I?

It's cold in here, causing my nipples to pebble against the fabric of my shirt. Soon after, the hand grazes my sensitive buds, pinching them. I don't want to like it, but my depraved mind does.

Panic claws at my insides, ripping me open as I fight with everything I have to get away.

"Stop fighting it, angel. I'm never letting you go now."

His hand tightens around my throat, fingers digging into my skin. My pulse races erratically beneath his touch, a concoction of anxiety, panic, and fear blending through my veins.

No, no, no, I chant in my head, willing myself to wake up from this nightmare. It can't be him. It can't fucking be him.

But of course it is. I defied his orders, and now I'm facing the consequences.

As my shorts slip off my legs, a warm breath brushes against my entrance, sending goosebumps all over me. I instinctively try to squirm away as the pleasure wreaks havoc on my body when I feel something meet my clit, and an involuntary moan escapes my lips.

This isn't a dream. Viper is behind me, tongue teasing my sensitive spot. Confusion makes me struggle to differentiate between nightmare and reality because I know it's his voice coming from behind me, pressing me toward the bed and preventing my movements.

"What?" I voice, only causing him to chuckle once more.

It's a sound I've grown accustomed to during all the times I tried to ignore him during our encounters leading up to the heist.

Where am I now? I'm sure as fuck not in my apartment. Has the fucker kidnapped me, taken me against my will, and now he's…licking me?

"You taste like the most delicious meal I've ever had," he growls, his voice too erotic in my intoxicated mind. "I told you to meet me at the cliffs, but you were a bad fucking girl, Arcane." He takes a deep breath. "So, I brought you to them instead."

His touch sends shivers down my spine, but I refuse to succumb to the pleasure he's coaxing from my body. What is Viper doing here? More importantly, why?

My mind is in a daze, unable to grasp the situation as he licks me. Curses and worries fly out the window the minute I reach my climax, and he drinks in every single ounce of it.

The moment the pleasure dissipates, I summon a final surge of energy to break free, scrambling up the bed. Dizziness overtakes me, the room spinning, but before I can confront Viper behind me, to see his face clearly, he forcefully pushes my head against the wall, leaving me with no choice but to oblige.

"Now, now, little angel. You're not allowed privileges."

I move to scream, needing to put as much distance between us as possible despite being tied to a fucking bed. He is the enemy, for fuck's sake, the harbinger of death from a rivaling family who has come to take me.

Oh God. What have I done?

The moment he must feel I'm about to scream, his glove-free hand covers my mouth, preventing the sounds from escaping.

A growl tears from his throat. "Scream all you want. There's no one for miles to hear you."

Slowly, he eases the pressure on my head, and I turn toward him as the silken bands dig into my wrists, seeing his eyes full of conflicting emotions. He's right; screaming won't get me anywhere, mainly because of the waves crashing outside, their echoes plunging the world into a terrible wonder. A storm is brewing, coming to bring death and destruction, as two descendants from rivaling families meet.

He assesses me, his words whispering against my ear. "If I untie your hands, do you promise not to scream?" He gives me a serious look.

I look at him, then nod, allowing him to untie the bands holding me captive to the headboard. As soon as my other hand is freed, I sink my teeth into his palm pressed taut against my mouth. It makes him groan as he recoils, waving his hand as if to alleviate the pain. Using the momentary reprieve, I slip my remaining hand from its silken restraint and bolt toward the door, hastily pulling up my shorts. My heart is a relentless beat in my chest as I reach for the handle.

Before I can grip it, his voice cuts through the air like razor blades, freezing me in place as if a wind from the Antarctic has swept through the space.

"Running won't save you, Arcane," he sneers. "You're mine,

and there's nowhere you can hide from me. Nowhere in the world where I wouldn't find you."

He advances toward me, and I turn to face his mask-covered expression, my hand still reaching for the door handle. My thoughts are scrambling, trying to figure out the situation.

"Why am I here, Viper?"

Somehow, as he hears the name, his body flinches—a slight motion that I would have missed had I closed my eyes. It makes my brow furrow, waiting for his response, analyzing his reactions as he scrutinizes mine.

We're like two predators, trying to figure out who is the most dangerous one, who's going to attack or flee first.

He takes another step closer, yet still far away, even as the interior reveals itself to be a cottage of some sort—not solely one room.

"I've already told you, you're mine," he merely states, a simple sentence yet laden with so many unspoken words.

"It doesn't make sense. None of it makes sense. We've met, what? Like a few times. Are you fucking insane?" My voice takes on a higher tone, and I watch as the anger slowly, gradually comes forth within him.

He clenches his fists, veins and mouthwatering tattoos prominent as the hoodie slides up his arms. He's the same height as me, yet in this moment, it feels as if he looms before me while stalking closer. With uncertainty gripping me, my hand gravitates toward the handle, slowly turning it.

He seems to contemplate my words for a few seconds. "Devil angel," he says, a silent warning and a reminder, causing my heart to crash inside me.

Those words are far too familiar, words I don't even want to remember.

"You killed all those guards. You've been following me. I don't belong to you. What the fuck, Viper?" I scream at him.

Anger radiates from me in waves as I desperately try to forget those two words he uttered. My breathing becomes labored.

"I did it because you're *mine*," he roars. "I will kill anyone who touches you."

"You don't even fucking know me!"

My throat stings from the shrillness of my voice, and I clench the handle behind me even tighter, the sensation of metal cooling my palm.

An amused smirk stretches his lips, his anger evaporating from his demeanor with no trace of it, as if it were never there to begin with.

"Oh, how wrong you are, little sister."

Chapter 15
Arcane

HIS WORDS ECHO IN the recesses of my mind, haunting me with their taunts. He might as well have dragged a knife through my heart, tearing through flesh and bone to reach it, before carving it out and tossing it over the edge of the cliffs outside. Acid rises in my throat, leaving a sour burn.

He stands there menacingly with his shoulders relaxed and arms slumped to the sides—casual. How isn't he more unnerved by this?

He's lying.

He cocks an eyebrow while waiting for my reaction, but I avoid his gaze, swiping mine over the cottage to find something I can use against him. He probably thinks I pose no threat to him, might believe his words got to me, making me reconsider my actions. Well, like I said, he doesn't fucking know me.

"I don't know who you are." My words are nearly drowned by the waves outside.

If I repeat those words enough times, they will ring true, and I will no longer feel as if I'm suffocating. Scanning the room, I see a gun—my gun—on top of the drawer closest to me.

His eyes land on it, his stance rigid as he looks at me with a narrowed gaze, waiting for the moment I will strike and he will chase.

Seconds pass as I remain unmoving, finally coming to a decision. Without another moment to spare, I beeline for the gun, grabbing it before turning the handle, slipping out to the windy world outside—away from the memories dredging up within.

I keep running, the storm intensifying. To my horror, I realize I'm farther away than I've ever been before, not recognizing my surroundings, especially not the small cottage behind me. But it's undeniably the cliffs I've been to for years, grieving the person I lost and who I used to be.

Glancing back, I see him advancing with angered, resolute strides. Every muscle screams as I push my legs to their limits. Surrounding us, only barren lands stretch for miles, with nowhere to hide in sight. Relentless waves crash against the cliffside, allowing rain to spray over me, and harsh winds impede my process.

The tumultuous cacophony of the wind and waves wreaks

inside my eardrums, masking any sound of Viper's pursuit behind me. A glimmer of hope ignites as the scattered trees gradually thicken the deeper into the woods I come. Slowing my pace, I risk a glance over my shoulder.

He's gone.

I stagger toward a sturdy tree, seeking refuge as I lean against its trunk. Adrenaline and fear shoot through my body, a lethal concoction threatening to rob me of precious oxygen and plunge me into a dizzying feeling of faintness. Casting another apprehensive glance over my shoulder, I find no sign of him amidst the storm.

Didn't he chase me at all? I'm certain I heard someone trailing behind me, but the tempestuous weather made it hard to be sure.

Scrambling to reach the phone he miraculously left in my leather jacket pocket, I clutch the gun in my other hand, desperation urging me forward. I fumble to unlock my phone before I locate Alec's saved contact, knowing he'll always have my back as my best friend.

Before I can dial, it clutters to the ground, and an ominous presence stands before me. A mask covers his face, commanding my attention with a chilling touch. A suffocating lump lodges in my throat like an immovable stone. I'm all alone, with no one for miles to save me.

"There's nowhere you can hide from me, devangel. I will find you. Every. Goddamn. Time," he growls, squeezing my already aching throat.

Wide-eyed, I stare at him, terror slithering through me like a fiery torrent.

Eventually, fear gives way to anger, radiating through me in waves. Summoning every ounce of strength, I use the self-defense techniques taught by the Valentis to kick at his leg, causing him to groan and step back. The brief reprieve allows me to push him away, raising the gun to his forehead. Despite my best efforts, I can't hide the tremors racking my body, or how I'm crumbling apart on the inside.

Oh God.

I feel sick. The sickening wave of truth threatens to overwhelm me as if I might spill the contents of my stomach.

The realization hits me like a sledgehammer—he can't be here, it can't be true. He's supposed to be dead. He *died* five fucking years ago, leaving me to fend for myself. *Oh fucking God.*

He glares as I aim the gun, adjusting my stance for stability. The wind whips around us, even amidst the dense trees. I can't afford to waver for one second, or it will shatter my resolve. His demeanor is infuriatingly cocky, and even if his face remains hidden behind the mask, the familiarity of his arrogance makes memories come rushing back. I'm seconds away from pulling the trigger, but despite my determination, my hands tremble too much, making it impossible for me to get a good aim. *I'm going to fucking puke.*

His betrayal pushes down on me as if a monster has come to drag me to the depths of hell. I'm forced to keep steady, even as the coldness of the wind makes me shiver.

"Put down the gun," he calmly says, yet there's nothing in his voice to indicate that he's the least bit threatened about this.

But of course, he's the notorious biker, the current leader of the García cartel, who's ruthless. He isn't the same as then, but he's still a liar who went on his merry little way and left me to die at the hands of our foster parents when they couldn't stand me anymore.

I don't drop the gun, causing his gorgeous brown eyes to narrow into two slits.

"You're supposed to be dead," I whisper, desperately trying to keep my voice steady, but it's all too fucking much.

How many times have I stood by these cliffs, screaming out my agony, crying and raging from betrayal and longing?

"You lied to me," I say, rage making my voice tremble. "You said you'd never hurt me."

A laugh tears from my throat, realizing how pathetic I was growing up—putting my entire heart in his hands to hold and protect.

Anger seeps through his soul, staining his skin with an ominous hue, like ink spilled upon a pristine canvas. *This is it,* I think. This is the true him, the one who wouldn't allow anyone to threaten him or his position. The foster brother who'd laugh as I hurt myself, yet made me feel safe during thunderstorms. Each breath he takes seems to smolder with wrath. His eyes hold a lethal glint as he stares at my gun expectantly, wanting me to drop it.

The distant roar of waves echoes from behind, blending with the haunting whistles of wind through the trees. Something appears to consume his mind until his gaze flickers on the fallen phone, its screen dimming until going dark. It was enough for him to see the person I'd attempted to call. A ferocious tide crashes against the shores of his composure.

"Do you have any idea who they are? They're monsters!" he shouts, voice raw with emotions.

His words don't make sense because he's the one working with my found family. Anger consumes me as I shout at him, thrusting the gun's barrel into his chest. "They're not monsters, you are! You abandoned me. You. Left. Me."

I'm torn apart just by the sight of Kaiden—Viper—making me want to forget this ever happened.

This can't be real. Soon, I'll wake up, safe in my bed, and this erotic nightmare will be over.

But as I open my eyes again, he's still there, a painful reminder of all I've lost.

I step back, still aiming the gun at him. "You're supposed to be fucking dead!"

He flinches, and something unknown passes his face while he waits for my next move. With resolve, I erase all emotions from my expression, focusing solely on the target before me.

This is the only way because I'm still not certain that this isn't a dream. Taking a deep breath, I focus, my finger on the trigger. I have to rid myself of the devil who's haunted me for five agonizing years. There's no way out other than death.

My finger pushes against the trigger, but I fail to comprehend his swiftness as his body abruptly presses me against a tree, expelling the air from my lungs. The shot goes off, reverberating through the trees as it hits a trunk farther away, missing my intended target.

The power in his muscles is evident as he rips off his mask. He's fucking stunning in a way that steals my breath away yet fills me with regret for laying my eyes on him. Beautiful in a way that conjures memories of our past together, remembering all our shared moments.

He's fuming, quickly disarming me before pressing the gun against me. "You're mine," he snarls.

Stunned, I watch as he lowers his hand to my shorts, dragging them down my knees. "Not a day has passed where I haven't yearned to be with you. To possess you. I never let you go, not for a moment in all these years." His words are dangerously low.

As if oblivious to my disdain, he shoves my panties aside, slipping a finger inside me. I scream out in a tumult of surprise, pleasure, and hatred.

"I love the way you scream," he taunts, adding another finger.

"I should kill you," I grit out, but he only chuckles, his hair in disarray.

"Too bad I have the gun, then. Lucky for me." His lips stretch into a cruel smirk, dragging the weapon toward my mouth. With the barrel pressed against my lips, his next words freeze me in place.

"Suck on the gun like the good girl I know you are."

I'm about to protest, but he inserts the muzzle into my mouth, fear rendering me motionless.

I don't recognize this man anymore.

His other hand finds my clit, rubbing it as he demands I hollow my cheeks around the weapon, pushing it deeper until it hits the back of my throat. Despite my revulsion, an undeniable arousal takes hold. I reluctantly suck on the gun—he leaves me no choice—and watch his cock press against his pants. The outline of it makes me salivate.

He pulls out the gun, touching my clit with it. Every instinct screams at me to stop him, terrified as I am. But deep down, I know I don't want him to stop. If this is a fucked-up dream where I can have him again in any way, I want to savor the moment because this fantasy will vanish when I wake up.

The metal pushes against me, making panic take over, yet I can't resist when he guides it past my folds, easing it inside me with a brutality that's both painful and pleasant.

"So fucking beautiful. You've always been," he coos, freeing his cock with his other hand.

My eyes bulge at the sight of his hardness, heightened by the piercings that weren't there before.

As if sensing my question, he chuckles. "Got it a year ago, knowing I'd make you mine again."

"I'm not yours," I retort, but my words are silenced when he buries the barrel inside me, making me suck in a sharp breath. I hate myself for enjoying this.

"We know that's a lie, little sister. Spread your legs," he commands. "I want to see how your gun slips inside you. Show your brother how much he owns his sister."

I shouldn't feel as turned on as I do when I hear him calling us sister and brother, but I am. It's embarrassing at the same time as it's arousing. I gasp when he rotates the gun, causing pleasure unlike anything else. While he strokes his cock, I'm immobilized, too scared and aroused to respond in any way except to enjoy the sensations he compels me to experience.

I shouldn't allow this. But then he hits a deep spot inside me, and I cry out from the sharp pleasure, black spots dancing in my vision. His mouth latches onto my neck, sucking, biting, marking me for all to see, as if he never left.

"Please stop," I beg him, but I don't want him to.

"Please *don't* stop? Okay, angel," he smirks against my mouth, forcing his tongue inside as he continues to fuck me with the gun.

My legs tremble, my body leaning against the tree trunk to keep balance. I curse myself for how quickly this escalated, but as he kisses me in a bruising hold, I'm taken back to the life I once had, the woman I used to be.

He stimulates my clit with one hand while the other holds the gun inside me. The awful realization that the gun is loaded hits me, knowing he could kill me if he pulled the trigger. Yet, I know he wouldn't.

Tears well in my eyes. I fucking missed him, and I despise that so much it feels as if I might die, but it's the truth. He angles the gun, bringing me to the edge, prompting a loud moan from me. He groans as he leaves my clit and strokes his cock, muscles tensing.

"Scream louder for me as you come," he urges, and I comply.

My back arches against the tree, my body strung tight with desperation as he works the gun faster, prolonging the orgasm until I'm begging him to stop. I feel myself squirting, leaving me breathless when he withdraws it from me. Sweat coats his forehead as he works himself to orgasm, releasing all over my stomach. He brings the gun to his lips, licking it clean, and my heart constricts.

He's so different now, yet still the same Kaiden I knew, and it overwhelms me. My hand traces his cheek, its contours beautifully sharp.

He stiffens at first, the underlying rage gradually subsiding until he relaxes in my hold. I study his eyes, and by the way he responds to my touch, it's as if he hasn't been touched in five years. My heart aches when he lets out a satisfied hum.

"I thought you were dead," I whisper, and he rests his forehead against mine, inhaling deeply as if reveling in my presence.

"I know," he sighs.

Emotions flood over me—heartbreak, pain, anger, the yearning for death. And then I surrender to the tears, allowing myself to feel something in the presence of another, as I let him hold me while I cry.

Chapter 16
Arcane

THE RAIN TAPS PERSISTENTLY against the windows, leaving relentless trails as I struggle to process my thoughts as he begins to speak. His voice cuts through the air, yet it's devoid of remorse or empathy, contrasting with the turmoil within me.

"I can't tell you I'm sorry because I'm not," he declares, tone cold and unyielding. I tense, bracing myself for the rest. "I left you and had no choice but to fake my own death because it was necessary for my survival. If I'm dead, there's no protecting you," he growls, eyes flashing with a dangerous intensity. "I needed you alive, regardless of the consequences."

His confession sends a wave of conflicting emotions I cannot make sense of. Anger radiates from him like a searing heat, but beneath it, I sense the torment churning within his heart of stone. His eyes, though cold, flare with lust, and I'm unsure of how to react as I stare at him.

"Louis García revealed I was his blood and expected me to take over the García cartel after my biological brother died. I couldn't get back to you—his damn associates kept eyes on me at all times."

His clenched fists betray his emotions, and I recognize the powerlessness he must have felt in that moment. A man so in control, losing it within a day, watching everything fall apart around him.

"Until Lous García died in a gang war," Viper concludes. "I should thank the criminal world we live in for ridding me of my remaining biological relatives I never even wanted. But now, I finally have you."

The hardships he's faced, the grim truth of being thrust into the underworld as an heir to a notorious family—it's all too much. My heart aches for him, though he'd kill me if I ever admitted that out loud.

He never died. For years, he's been in the same town as me without my knowledge. *Why didn't he find me sooner?*

Amidst my inner turmoil, I'm anchored to the spot, his eyes roaming over my body as if he can't get enough. His shirtless form is illuminated by the descending sun outside, chest adorned with tattoos. One stands out—an *A*—and he catches me staring at it, speechless. Another bears the García family's mark, while the rest hold significance only to him.

A pang of longing pierces me, and despite sitting before me, he feels a hundred miles away. Years of brutality have led me to this moment: facing the one who inflicted the greatest torment. For years, I sought revenge for his abandonment, but now my world is tilted on its axis.

How do I move on from this? I can't simply dismiss everything we've endured together. A part of me yearns for him, craving him after being deprived for so long. I hate it.

"Why didn't you come find me?" I ask, my despair vaguely hidden.

After hours of sharing our stories, we're both emotionally and physically drained. We've both faced hardships, but I'm unsure if I can ever truly move past this.

I want to. Oh, do I want to. But can I give myself to him? The way he looks at me suggests I may not have a choice. I don't know if I should flee again or stay grounded. Perhaps I secretly enjoy the chase.

After a tense silence, he finally responds. "They threatened to harm you if I didn't comply. You're my weakness and they exploited it. It wasn't until Louis García's death and my ascension to the throne that I gained the freedom to do whatever I wanted. But don't worry, I never left your side."

His words leave me stunned, and before I can reply, he interrupts, eyes hardened and chest heaving.

"I couldn't shake you from my thoughts, and it was driving me mad!"

Suddenly, he's on his feet, prowling toward me. I step back, feeling like prey before the predator. He's always been the one I fear, yet it's an emotion that ignites a primal heat between my legs.

Before I can process what's happening, he pins me against the wall with a choking hold.

"Fucking make it stop!" he roars, squeezing harder as I claw at his hand, and yet I feel my lower stomach tingling, drenching my panties.

I remain silent as he pauses, lost in thought. My pulse races as he guides me to a table, pressing me against its surface. I can't understand his plans.

"Please, Viper. Let's talk about it," I plead.

"There's no talking about it," he mutters. "I was gone for five goddamn years, and I'll never get them back. But I have to make amends."

Reaching for the chains I hadn't noticed beside the table, he secures my wrists to the table legs, the metallic clinks echoing in the room whilst my back is pressed against the surface. I gasp as he cuts through my panties with a knife, a twisted glint in his eyes. At the sight of the knife, I fight against the restraints while grasping for any semblance of control.

"There's no running, little sister."

"The Valentis will know I'm gone!" I insist, hoping to sway his resolve.

"The Valentis are pieces of shit, unworthy of anyone's trust in the underworld. They're outcasts with no allies."

"That's not true," I argue, desperation clutching my tone.

"Don't trust any family in Penumbra Crest. We need to find and destroy the drive to ensure our survival. Understand?"

Uncertainty clouds my judgment. How can I trust him after all this time? Yet, deep down, my soul draws to his in ways it never has with anyone else. It used to be us against everything else, and a part of me longs for that connection again.

When I don't instantly respond to his subtle question, his hand strikes my breast, causing me to gasp from the unexpected sensation. A cruel smirk dances across his lips as he admires every inch of me, keeping me cuffed and vulnerable.

The cold air brushes my exposed pussy, sending a tremor through me as he unfastens his belt. I stifle the rising panic as he cuts open my shirt with his knife, wondering about his motives.

He tosses aside the torn fabric, and the frigid blade delicately tears through my flesh, blood coating my skin, reminiscent of what he did to my shoulder blade. I quiver against the cool touch of metal. The sensation of being laid open like this overwhelms me, leaving me flushed, especially as he grabs the knife and licks it clean, just as he did with the gun.

"So beautiful, all chained up for your brother's mercy," he groans, removing his belt, pants, and boxers, his cock springing free, adorned with two piercings at the top. With the blade pressed against my nipple, I tremble as he glides it gently across my chest to the other, hardening both buds as I lay on top of the table.

He stands between my legs, and I want to close them for

protection, but they're locked up. He leans down, his breath teasing my folds, making my pussy crave his touch.

"Why do you think I'll work with you again after this?" I ask.

"Because you want revenge just as much as I do for their abandonment," he grits out as if the thought itself physically pains him.

"Please don't," I beg.

"I love it when you beg for me." Without further notice, he dives between my legs, his tongue licking until I'm arching my back with a hitched breath.

Right before I'm close to coming, he withdraws his mouth, moving to stand before me. His cock points outward as it brushes against my lips.

"Do you trust me?" he asks, cock teasing me.

"No," I shake my head, uncertain yet too turned on.

"Good," he smirks. "Swallow your foster brother's cock."

Forced to accept him, I part my lips as he thrusts inside. His hand finds my nipple, and from somewhere behind him, he retrieves two nipple clamps, adjusting them onto my buds. Gasping and panting, I'm unable to draw in proper breaths with his cock stuffing my mouth.

"That's it."

I can't resist as he drives his cock deeper into my mouth and throat, making me gag as saliva drips from the corners. With each forceful thrust, he seeks the pleasure he denied me by withholding my release. Moaning around his length, his hand finds my clit, intensifying the sensations as his cock pushes deeper into my throat.

As I approach my climax, his fingers pump inside me at a torturous rate.

"Can you swallow my cum?" he asks, though it's a rhetorical question.

In the next second, he comes down my throat, fingering me until I'm coming all over his fingers, moans stifled by his cock in my mouth. When he pulls out, I'm breathless, nipples and pussy weeping, coated in sweat and blood.

"Are you more comfortable working on this heist with me now?" he inquires, raising an eyebrow.

"No, but I'm going to do it anyway. For my own sake," I declare, and he solemnly nods.

I have to work with him, if only for my own peace of mind. Despite the eternal sorrow and anger he's caused, they have somehow morphed into something else—all because of one person I shouldn't ever want to see again.

But the thing is, I do want him. No matter how much he's fucked up, my twisted mind still longs for him.

"Good enough. We should start preparing."

Resolute in my decision, I nod, steeling myself for the revenge I've longed for, though now for entirely different reasons.

Chapter 17
Viper

I'VE NEVER BEEN A good person, preferring to balance on the thread of complete blackness, and when I saw her covered in blood yesterday, my heart hammered inside my ribcage until my cock twitched painfully.

She's fucking intoxicating, and I can't wait to see the fury simmer beneath her skin when she awakens, realizing what I have in store for her.

Nestled on a carpet at the far end of the open cottage—purchased with the fortune I inherited from Louis García—her naked form slumps against the floor with only a thin blanket covering her legs, leaving her curves exposed to my hungry gaze.

Nipple clamps are fastened on her buds, and a collar encircles her throat, tethering her to the cage enveloping her. It's human-sized, designed to confine her to a seated position and restrict her movements.

Her nipples are hard from the cool air, but I've already stoked the fire in the fireplace, so it'll be warm soon enough. She's out cold after I drugged her water yesterday. Even now, my cock strains against my sweatpants as I look at her. Patience has never been my virtue, especially when it comes to her.

I perch on the chair before the cage with a relaxed posture, crossing one leg over the other. My bare chest displays my tattoos, and I recall how her gaze lingered on the letter *A* inked into my skin, undoubtedly curious about its meaning. Yet, she never voiced her question aloud.

I had it tattooed the day I had to leave, as a memory and promise to never let her go, never stop fighting for what's ultimately mine.

Yesterday, we spent the night planning the upcoming heist. She sent a message to Alec Valenti—courtesy of me—assuring him she was okay and conserving her energy for the task ahead.

I wait, observing her vulnerable, beautiful frame inside the cage. When her eyes flutter open, a soft groan escapes her, stirring a primal desire that makes blood rush to my cock. I imagine she must be sore from sleeping on the hard floor.

As she reaches for her head, groaning with discomfort, she remains oblivious to the collar and leash restraining her.

Her eyes adjust to the dimness, and she slowly sits up, only to bump her head against the cage's metallic roof, causing her to hiss out a breath. I chuckle involuntarily, and her eyes snap to mine. There's a shift in the atmosphere, tension crackling between us. Her eyes flicker to my gloved hand resting atop my knee, a flicker of something unknown passing over her features. Perhaps she remembers how I got the scars marring my hand, and why I cover them with gloves.

She rubs her eyes, blinking away the remnants of her tiredness until her surroundings come into focus. Her gaze darts around the cottage, noticing the bars encircling her within the cage.

She sits up faster this time, careful not to hit her head as she wraps the blanket around herself. She crawls toward the metal bars nearest to me, the clinking of the collar and leash serving as a testament to her confinement. Her eyes smolder with unseen rage, knuckles whitening from the harsh grip in which she grips the bar.

"What the fuck, Viper?" she growls. I can almost envision tiny puffs of smoke emanating from her ears.

A smirk tugs at my lips, cruel and taunting, as I meet her fiery gaze with an air of nonchalance. Seeing her react like this over something I caused is kind of…*cute.*

"I couldn't risk you running away again until I know for sure you won't leave." My voice is calm and unbothered as I grab a glass of water from the table and take a sip. I extend it toward her, but she shakes her head, the stubborn woman.

"So you decided to lock me in a cage?"

I shrug indifferently. "You look so pretty all locked up."

Her chest heaves with humiliation, and she desperately looks around, trying to find a way out of there. She won't find one without my permission. There's only one key.

She leans her head against the bars, closing her eyes as if fighting nausea. I might have given her too many sleeping pills.

"The drugs should be wearing off any second now."

"You fucking drugged me?" She attempts to push and pull on the bar, but they're steadfast, unmoving.

"I couldn't risk waking you."

"I'll fucking kill you," she pointlessly warns, knowing damn well I'm not threatened by her.

"You will crawl and beg for me, too. Don't throw empty threats you can't uphold." I look at her as I stand from the chair, crouching beside the cage as my hand strokes her cheek tenderly.

She unconsciously leans against it before quickly gaining self-awareness. That's when I grab her throat through the cage, making her whimper, and something feral comes alive inside me. I cut off the oxygen entering her lungs, and she looks at me with a kind of lust that begs me to fuck her, even if she's too stubborn to admit it.

"I'll never beg you."

"We'll see about that," I challenge, tugging on the leash attached to her collar, forcing her even closer to the bars.

Her breasts are pressed against the cold metal, and she lets out another whimper, her cheeks flushed with untold desire.

With my leather-clad hand, my finger prods her lips until they instinctively open. She squirms, her thighs pressing together as if I make her all fuzzy.

She sucks on my finger, and I can't help but let out a growl of something dark, only to be interrupted by the sharp pain of her bite. I hiss, pulling my hand back and glaring at her. Now, it's her turn to smile triumphantly at me, like a lioness thinking she's won—it only makes me want to dominate her further.

"I warned you."

I hum, feeling a thrill through me as I pull out the knife from my pocket, inching closer to her. With the leash in one hand, I guide her to the edge of the small cage, the glint of the blade barely grazing her skin, drawing a small trickle of blood. She tries to move away, but I keep her in place.

Watching the blood trickle down her leg, I crave more, envisioning her bathed in blood—a gorgeous fucking sight—but I remind myself that I need her alive more than I need her dead. She's my hell and heaven wreaking havoc over my soul. My devangel.

Pulling the leash, she's forced onto all fours, struggling to breathe as I tie the end of it to a hook beside the cage. With her trapped in place, I walk to the other side, taking in the sight of her pussy on full display for me. The confinement of the cage forces her legs apart, and she's fucking dripping.

My depraved little devil.

There's a hitch in her breath when she fights to get out of the cage once more. "Let me out," she whispers, but I ignore her. "Please, let me out." Her voice quivers, but I'm drawn to her vulnerability, relishing the power I hold over her.

Ignoring her continuous pleas, I strip away my sweatpants and boxers, knowing that while she might struggle to breathe in the confined space, she's soaked for me, nearly staining the blanket beneath. My cock springs free, and I stroke it leisurely, watching her grind her hips against the air. Her pink pussy is exposed, making her all the more sensitive, goosebumps spreading over her body. She craves my touch, yearning for the stimulation only I can offer.

Reaching between the bars, I adjust her position so her pussy and ass are on full display for me, the chain tightening its hold and making her gasp for breath. I dip a finger inside her, and she moans unabashedly. Her reaction betrays her initial fear when desire takes over, and instead of succumbing to panic from the enclosed space, she eagerly grinds her hips against my hand, craving more.

Pre-cum leaks from my tip, close to where my two piercings are, and I'm unable to resist anymore. I get on my knees, positioning her hips so her ass is in the air, allowing me access. Desire pulsates through me as I prod her entrance, and inch by inch, she takes me. I thrust into her, filling her up until she's moaning and whimpering, begging for more while pleading to be let out of the cage.

Fuck. It feels so good to be inside her again, like driving home after so long.

"You're taking me so well," I moan out, thrusting faster, driving deeper inside her until she nearly falls over inside the cage, but the leash and collar keep her upright. "You think you can take a finger in that pretty asshole?" I don't give her a chance to reply.

I spit down onto her asshole, the saliva acting as a lubricant as I carefully insert a finger inside her. She clenches tightly around my digit, her moans growing louder as I continue to fuck her through the cage.

"Don't think we're over after this heist," I threaten.

She's unable to reply because her delicate moans mingle with sniffles, revealing her conflicted emotions about everything transpiring around us. She shudders in my hold, her climax building rapidly. I quicken my pace, causing her to reach the peak of pleasure, dragging me along with her. My chest heaves with exertion, my obsession for her only growing stronger.

"Fuck. You're so fucking delicate when you come."

"I still hate you," she stutters out, her eyes glazing over and breathing quickening. "You're a monstrous grave that sent me to my ruin and shattered everything I was. But I can't let you go." I swear I see a tear trickle down her cheek, and my shoulders instantly stiffen, not knowing how to handle her emotions. "For so long, I tried to forget about you. You're like a disease, pestering inside me until I have no choice but to oblige."

"I take that as a compliment," I mutter, locking eyes with her.

In that instant, I vow to never let her go ever again. She's fucking mine.

Chapter 18
Arcane

MY BREATH IS VISIBLE in the chilly night air, creating small puffs of smoke as I peer into the darkness of the biggest dock owned by the Grimaldis. My fingers itch to get started, with anticipation thrumming through every nerve ending in my body. I've waited for this moment since my twenty-first birthday, and it's finally within my grasp. Revenge has weighed heavily on my shoulders for years, and now, as I stand on the precipice of achieving it, I'm not sure what will push me forward when all is over. If there'll be anything left of me beyond this thirst for vengeance.

With the stolen sonar equipment, we found the submarine nestled in the treacherous waters surrounding Penumbra Crest. It's carrying a valuable USB drive with stolen data that could unravel the balance of power among the criminal families. Our mission is to destroy it before the Grimaldis and Ivanovas lay claim to it, thus jeopardizing the already fragile truce that maintains order among us all.

In that drive lies sensitive information of everyone involved, posing a great threat. Its exposure would not only destroy all innocent citizens' lives but also rage war upon us all.

Every cell in my body is on high alert, trembling with the onslaught of nerves eating me alive. It's not that I'm scared; it's that everything has to go according to the plan. This is my one shot at revenge, and frankly, freedom.

Adjusting the straps of my duffel bag, I climb off my black bike, awaiting instructions from Alec in my earpiece. The weight of my weapons and the tungsten carbide drill press against my back. Glancing down at the dock, I observe the guards strategically positioned. They won't see us coming. We've bided our time meticulously, ensuring every aspect is flawlessly executed.

"I know you're well-acquainted with the plan." Alec's voice is loud in my ear. "Our associates will meet you at the dock. I'll oversee the security systems while Viper is stationed outside, providing overwatch with his scope until you give him the clear to enter the warehouse."

I nod, even if he can't see me, determination fueling my body. *Bring it on.*

"Proceed through the back entrance, where two guards are

positioned," Alec continues. "Access the safe room, utilize the drill to breach it, and install our surveillance system for access. Await Viper's arrival, then take the speedboat to the submarine. Our associates will secure the front and come after you as backup."

"Understood."

With my tools secured, I make my way toward the dock, ensuring my knife is tucked into my combat boot, and my gun is within reach. The past years have been a hassle, with the despair of losing a part of who I was, my family, and my foster brother. Yet, the last few days spent with Viper—no matter how fucked up he is, and that he kidnapped me—have given me a glimmer of hope. Maybe I can mend the wounds of the past and find solace in the future, but it requires a lot of personal growth from within.

Viper. The mere thought of him being alive feels like a sharp blade piercing my chest, yet it's also a comforting bandage wrapped around a wound.

With us finally working together, I've gathered all the information he obtained, including the stolen schematics I sought a few weeks ago. Earlier this morning, I met up with Alec and his cousins, and we destroyed the Grimaldis' weaponry storage, leaving them more vulnerable than ever before.

The stench of cigarette smoke overwhelms me as I come to the back of the dock, the large warehouse looming before me. Used cigarettes lay scattered on the ground, with ash littering the gravel—some guards were just here smoking. I steel myself, focusing steadily.

I've been on multiple missions since joining the Valentis, taught how to defend myself and defeat enemies. This heist isn't something unusual, but it's bigger, more important.

"I'm approaching the back door," I whisper into my mic, hoping both Alec and Viper can hear me.

Making sure the coast is clear, I pray Alec has successfully disarmed the security alarms as my hand reaches for the door handle. With a silent exhale of relief, I crack it open, a small smile tugging at my lips when no alarm sounds, giving me unhindered access to the warehouse. My footsteps reverberate through the stone walls as I navigate through the empty corridor, my senses sharp while keeping an eye out for any sign of danger. Somewhere far ahead, the soft pattering of water droplets cascading down a drain fills the space.

My heart pounds against my ribcage as I press on. I've studied this building and its blueprints for months, memorizing every nook and cranny. Ahead and to the left in the corridor are the first two guards, and as I make my way there, I see how they scan the surroundings while remaining focused on the door leading to the parking lot.

Grabbing my gun, I aim and shoot one of the guards with a precise shot to the head. His body crumples noiselessly to the ground, thanks to the silencer attached to my weapon. Before the other guard can process what happened, I swiftly shoot him as well, his lifeless form joining his colleague, blood pooling around their corpses.

With the rest of our associates handling the guards at the front, I focus on locating the safe room, before I signal to Viper that he can enter. The Grimaldis and Ivanovas are at the submarine, doing illegal business with the rat who stole and sold the drive and car.

"Incoming guard to the left." Alec's voice crackles in my ear, and I stand ready, pulling the trigger when a guard comes barreling forward—probably wondering why he can't get a hold of his colleagues.

I start rushing forward, feet hitting the stone floor as I turn right in the empty corridor, quickly locating the safe room. Three shots ring off in the distance, sounding like thunderous claps that vibrate through the space, and I can only assume it's the associates doing their job.

It doesn't take long until I find it, a door constructed of reinforced steel, made to keep the enemies out. At its center is a heavy-duty combination lock meant to confuse. Drawing the drill from my duffel, I steady my nerves and activate the tool, its shrill whirring filling the corridor. I know the guards will soon be alerted, so I work faster. As the drill bites into the lock, beads of sweat gather on my forehead, a surge of energy pumping through me. It feels like an eternity passes until I finally hear the satisfying click of the lock giving way. With my breath held, the door creaks open, revealing the secret passage leading to the cave where the speedboat awaits, ready to take us to the submarine.

I step into the room with its concrete walls and rows of shelves filled with rations and water bottles. A collection of weapons hangs from the walls. They've clearly prepared for any type of emergency, but too bad for them—I will shatter everything they hold dear.

There's a surveillance camera in the corner of the room, its red light blinking as if aware of me. I ignore its watchful gaze, approaching the large computer on a bench at the far end connected to the camera. Retrieving the same drive I used when I scoped out their dock, I quickly insert it into the computer. It only takes a minute before my phone emits a soft beep, indicating that I have successfully installed the system, granting me access to their security feeds.

While we can hack into their systems from the outside, the safe room requires a more hands-on approach. Here, we need to physically attach the drive to corrupt their systems.

The air inside the safe room becomes stale, with a faint scent of must and old metal, and I quickly remove the drive from their computer as I'm about to alert Viper. He has to come here now so we can move to the submarine together.

Pressing the right button on my earpiece, I connect myself to Viper and Alec, sharing the same communication line.

"It's all settled," I declare, awaiting one of their responses.

My skin prickles with shivers, and it feels as if a runaway train pushes through my skin. An impending doom hangs in the air, though I can't yet tell what it is.

Immediately, I grab my phone, ready to access the security

feed. Then, I see how all the screens are frozen on one time stamp, repeating in an endless loop. This wasn't part of the plan. Dread replaces the earlier relief I felt at having entered the safe room, and every cell in my body screams at me to get out as soon as possible.

My hands tremble as I try the earpiece again, desperately wanting to reach either Alec or Viper. I hate that I'm alone, and none of them replies, meaning I have to proceed by myself.

I quickly emerge through another door at the end of the safe room, coming into a small cave that's hidden deep behind the dock, away from prying eyes. The sun is just setting behind the horizon, leaving an ethereal glow that only makes this worse, knowing darkness will soon set.

I find the speedboat in the water of the cave, and my footsteps echo off the stone walls inside the cavern as I approach it. It bobs gently against the water, and I release the boat from its ropes, climbing aboard.

At first, I sit and wait for Viper to emerge through the door like we'd initially planned. Worry etches into my chest like a permanent tattoo. Why can't I get a hold of any of our associates?

There's only one thing I can do—I need to do it by myself. With a deep breath, I attempt to start the engine, firmly grasping the starter rope handle and steadily pulling it.

It doesn't work.

I repeat the process. Nothing happens. Panic fills me, my eyes widening as I realize I'm stuck.

I try again and again, but it refuses to start. Staring down at the screens on my phone again, praying I can at least see what's going on outside the safe room, I notice they're still on the same time stamp, looping and hiding the truth.

"Something is wrong," I say into my earpiece, hoping someone on the other side will hear me.

A crackling noise causes me to flinch involuntarily. The connection out here is horrible. Through the static, I discern Viper's husky voice faintly entering my ear. "What…it?"

"Where are you?" I ask while something tightens in my chest, reminding me too much of the feeling of worry.

I hate that I worry about him—I shouldn't worry about him. He left me to die, abandoned me, and made me believe he was dead. But somehow, my heart refuses to think rationally.

Silence ensues for minutes, with only the echo of the cave as the source of sound. For comfort, I reach for the gun tucked into the belt on my waist, and I hold it before me with such a tight grip that my knuckles turn white.

A crackle comes from my earpiece, but I can't determine what the person is saying. With my heart in my throat, I jump out of the speedboat, running back to the safe room again and knowing I need to get a better connection so I can communicate with Alec, Viper, and the rest of our organization.

"Viper? Alec?" My voice is unsteady, my chest heaving.

Still no reply.

I enter the safe room, not hearing anything from the earpiece as I make my way out. I keep my eyes trained on the empty corridor before me, speaking into the mic once more.

"Viper, can you hear me?"

A loud shot rings off in the distance, and I discern screeching wheels, only worsening this situation. What the fuck is going on?

From Viper's mic, I hear an even louder shot, causing his breath to hitch. I've never heard him so unnerved before—the notorious leader of the Garcías and the biker who never gets scared. I clench my teeth with such force that the metallic tang of blood floods my mouth.

Suddenly, Viper's voice rings loud and clear in my ear, a panicked tone mingled with anger that makes sweat bead on my forehead. "Arcane, get out of there as soon as fucking possible!"

"What's going on?" I can't keep my voice from quivering.

"They never fucking got here," he says until another screeching sound arrives, loud voices booming.

Far off in the distance, I hear the sound of Benjamin Valenti's voice, and another one that makes my heart sink to the bottom of my stomach—a voice I never wished to hear again. Peter Grimaldi, our foster father.

"Angel, they lied to you. They fucking lied to you." I hear the distress in his voice, which only has me spiraling into a panicked state of mind.

My ears ring, blood pulsating through me until all I can hear is a thudding sound, an ache spreading through my head.

"Get out of there!" Viper breaks through the fog in my ears, and I snap to attention.

I dash through the corridor toward the back exit where I entered. Only now, the guard's corpses are gone, with only their blood a testament to them ever having been there.

"Fuck," I whisper, pushing forward.

Right as I reach the exit, I run into something solid. I expect it to be Viper, but when my eyes look up, I see Viper held back by two heavily armed guards, his eyes trained on mine with a cold expression while hiding everything he feels. My body is crushed to the gravelly ground, and I meet the eyes of the man who condemned me to hell when he threw me out of his home.

Shit, shit, shit.

A voice comes from my earpiece, and it's not Viper's.

"I'm sorry, Arcane."

Alec's voice is steady and clear, though he doesn't sound sorry at all.

And then, everything turns black.

Chapter 19
Arcane

A SEEPING CHILL SETTLES in my marrow, my eyelids fluttering as the dimly lit room gradually appears. Heart in my throat, I attempt to sit up, only to realize my limbs are restrained by chains biting into my skin, cutting off the blood circulation.

Panic surges like a live wire through my veins as memories flood back in disjointed fragments—a near-success operation retrieving the drive from the submarine, only to realize Viper never made it into the building. A sledgehammer pounds in my skull, and I groan. A lethal concoction of emotions threatens to suffocate me.

What happened to him after the guards held him back? He appeared battered, hair ruffled with a split lip and bruises forming around his eye—signs of a fight having taken place.

"Angel, they lied to you. They fucking lied to you."

If I could, I would press my palm against my mouth to stem the tide of bile rising, but I can't. Nausea overtakes me, and vomit spews out of my mouth, splattering onto the floor by my feet. Tears brim the corners of my eyes as a heavy feeling settles in my gut.

The Valentis lied to me.

A single light bulb dangles from the ceiling, casting shadows in the barren room. Memories swirl like debris in the storm of my mind, making it hard to piece together. Yet, I vividly recall the unforgiving eyes of Peter Grimaldi looking at me with hatred and disgust. Years of neglect from him, of trying to fit into a family that never wanted me, have left me unable to shake the fear I felt standing before him.

I never thought I'd have to face him again, especially when I'm not the one punishing him. His stance, paired with a clenched jaw and eyes that pierced through me, made bile rise up my throat, as if I were nothing but a stain on his impeccable suit.

I try the chains, fruitlessly tugging at them in a desperate attempt to break free. The metallic bite of pain sears through my skin as the chains dig deeper, drawing blood.

Like a whisper carried on the wind, a soft voice breaks through the silence, making me startle. I whip my head around, trying to find the source, but darkness obscures my sight. Did I imagine the voice?

"It won't work," the voice says, tone filled with resignation.

"I've already tried getting out. It doesn't work."

Slowly emerging from the shadows is a woman, her hands bound tightly in front of her stomach, feet secured to the wall by iron hooks. Disheveled hair frames her face, giving her a crazed appearance, while a glint in her eyes hints at untold emotions and stories.

"It's impossible," she tells me.

"Who are you?" I demand, confusion marring my features.

She doesn't answer, her gaze locked on the ground as if lost in thought. Frustration wells inside me as I realize she offers no answers. Tearing my eyes from her, I scan the room for any means of escape, but I come up empty in this room of barren walls.

A whimper escapes me as I tug at the chains, ignoring the pain as they tear through flesh. Desperation fuels me until the pain becomes unbearable, and the realization that I won't get out of these godforsaken chains fills me.

"I told you so," the voice mutters, and I shoot her an annoyed glare.

THE CREAKING OF THE door from above snaps me back to consciousness, my heart racing instantly. Straining my ears for any sound, I'm met with silence, leaving me staring at the ceiling. Disorientation fills me, and I realize I must have woken up from sleep.

"They always come and go," the soft, feminine voice floats across the room, her eyes trained on mine.

She looks different now, her hair untangled without any visible dirt on her. A faint scent of soap lingers in the air, and I frown at her in confusion.

She sighs exasperatedly. "If you're obedient, they allow you to clean up."

Disbelief coats my words. "What the hell?"

She merely shrugs, as if this is an everyday occurrence for her.

"Who are you?" I press further, but she offers no response. "What brings you here then?" I try again, but her gaze remains fixed on her clean nails while avoiding mine.

"They came to collect a debt," she finally reveals.

Her words are cryptic, leaving me more confused than ever. There's a profound sadness in her eyes that reflects years of pain and suffering, mirroring my own struggles. I recognize that look—the anguish of pain etched into her soul.

"Do you know where we are?" She remains silent, retreating into her mind to escape the cruel reality we're in. "Hello?" I call out again.

Before she can reply, a loud noise echoes through the space, causing her to tense.

"Keep quiet and look down. Do not disobey them," she hisses, right before a man in uniform steps into the room.

His stance is imposing, sending a surge of fear racing through me like a violent thunderstorm as he approaches, each step like a doom to an inevitable confrontation. My eyes travel from his pointed shoes to his black slacks, giving way to a buttoned-up shirt. Finally, his face comes into view—features I never want to see again.

I flinch at the sight of my foster father's smirk, his expression conveying my insignificance, as if I'm about to be crushed like an ant in his path.

"Well, well. If it isn't my beloved Arcane," he sneers, crouching before me while belittling me with his cruel presence. "I knew I would one day see you again, daughter."

Without hesitation, I spit on his face, saliva dripping down his cheek. He backhands me just as quickly, my head snapping to the side while a fiery sting spreads across my cheek.

His eyes narrow into razor-sharp slits, but I maintain an indifferent expression, knowing that predators feast on fear, and I refuse to fuel the fire.

"Where am I?" I manage to ask, masking my emotions.

The laughter that follows is cruel and taunting. "Your pathetic 'family' betrayed you," he mocks. "You're alone, Arcane. No one cares about you, and no one would ever love you enough to stay."

His words cut deep, carving a wound in my soul. I hold myself perfectly still, refusing him the satisfaction of seeing my pain.

I trusted them, and they betrayed me.

Inside, I'm screaming from the agony tearing me apart, but on the outside, I merely blink at him.

"How?"

"I suspect you already know the 'how,' my darling daughter. You simply refuse to admit it. They've been working with us all along."

A heavy weight settles in my stomach, pressing on my lungs until it feels as if they will cave in and I'll never recover again. *This is it,* I think. This is the moment all of the pain from the past and present will catch up with me until there's nothing left of me but burnt ashes fluttering in the wind.

Mr. Grimaldi's gaze reveals the cruel intent behind this encounter—how he relishes in my suffering, whether through words or actions. But unlike before, he never touched me, only inflicting mental abuse.

"They've been betraying you, feeding us their secrets. Did you truly believe it was that easy? That I wouldn't have the foresight to tighten our security?" His voice drips with disdain.

All blood drains my face, and I fight to conceal the turmoil raging within when all I want to do is crumble apart.

"They're too greedy for power. And you were the price. I can't wait to fucking break you again. You thought you escaped, you little shit. But I won't let you get away again. You're mine to do with whatever I please, and you're going to obey your father," he spits in my face, and I can't hide the disgust evident in my expression.

"Fucking break me! You think I haven't been broken before? You think I haven't felt the abandonment? I don't fucking care anymore," I retort, truth lacing my words.

After dedicating years to seeking revenge, there's nothing left to lose. Taking down the Grimaldis was my last goal, and even if he breaks me, I will not crumble. I'll find a way to get back at them.

"Shut up," he growls, backhanding me once more.

Before I can react, I'm hauled to my feet, the chains biting into my flesh. A loud gasp escapes me from the pain, and my foster father grumbles in annoyance, unshackling the chains. I stumble, my legs unable to keep me upright, but he doesn't care.

I steal a glance at the woman in the room, her eyes filled with pity and worry as she watches me being dragged away.

My heart pounds vividly inside my chest as I'm led out of the room into the stone stairwell. Dread twists in my stomach, nausea churning within when I see exactly where we are.

The Grimaldi base.

Memories assault my senses that I have a hard time containing, pain rippling through every being of me until I can scarcely draw breath. I look around in terror, the walls of this place a reminder of the horror I endured, once believing in the love of a foster family who ultimately betrayed me.

I was pathetic.

Entering my foster father's office, I'm pushed against his desk, stripped of dignity as my shirt is torn away. Humiliation mingles with fear as I struggle to suppress tears, clinging to whatever composure I can muster against his cruelty.

"We'll have quite the time together, daughter. I'll love watching you break."

Fear grips me like a vise, suffocating me as memories threaten to pull me under into a swirling abyss of despair. It was here I endured countless reprimands and reminders of being a mere pawn in a game made and ruled by men.

Here, I found out about my foster brother's death.

I hear my foster father grab something from a shelf before he draws closer. His associates eye me with greed, their intentions evident.

Without forewarning, the first blow lands on my back, searing pain erupting through me and forcing a scream from my lips— giving them exactly what they want. The whip cracks through the air, lashing out like poison and igniting a wildfire across my shoulder blades. I bite down hard on my tongue, tasting blood and metal.

Again and again, the whip descends upon my back, each strike tearing through flesh and bone with merciless precision. My foster father's words cut deeper, slicing through the fragile walls I built around my heart. "No one has ever wanted you. Fucking no one."

Every part of me aches—my heart, my back, my soul. I wish I wasn't affected by his words.

Beaten within an inch of my life, I'm dragged back to the basement, meeting the eyes of the unknown woman. They're full of worry again, looking at me with an unreadable expression.

They don't bother chaining me again, knowing I'm too goddamn weak to try to escape.

DAYS PASS, MARKED ONLY by the woman's daily trips upstairs when she's allowed to shower. Today is the fourth day of my imprisonment here, enduring relentless torture at the hands of my foster father, Peter Grimaldi. They chained me again two days ago.

My eyes throb painfully, and every movement sends a wave of agony that threatens to make me faint. Everything hurts, and my vision is hazy as I slump against the floor, avoiding putting pressure on my back. Yet, there's only one thought crossing my mind—I have to escape because no one else will help me.

Glancing at the woman as she sleeps, her troubled breathing betrays the nightmares she must have.

Throughout the days we've spoken, I've learned that she's been captivated for over a month, taken as collateral for a debt owed to the Grimaldi family, but little else. There's a determination inside her—one I recognize in myself. It reveals she wants to survive and fight despite the horrors I glimpse etched into her eyes, like scars on her soul.

Yesterday, she told me that Saturdays are when Peter Grimaldi leaves the mansion to gamble at the Ivanovas', leaving only the associates to watch out for us. A plan has formed in my mind, one that will either fail or succeed. At this point, it doesn't matter.

On the morning of the sixth day, as the woman is led back into the basement by a Grimaldi made man, I notice she's freshly clean, but new bruises mar her skin, coloring her cheek green and purple. Blood drips down her fingers, landing on the floor, revealing two of her nails have been ripped off from her fingers. Anger boils within me at the sight, simmering just beneath the surface.

"Bitch," the made man snarls as he chains her to the wall again, making sure to step on her hand and making her whimper before quickly concealing that she even made a sound.

"Hey, asshole!" I shout at him, my head pounding, but it's now or never—now's my chance to get my hands on this forsaken family.

His eyes snap to mine. "What?" he snarls, coming over to me.

I meet his gaze with defiance, and he doesn't like that because he reaches out to grab me in a bruising hold. I grit my teeth, feeling the woman's eyes on me, and for a moment, I meet them while the made man is busy staring me down. She has a broken piece of a mirror in her hand, and giving me a silent nod, she scoots it over to me.

Summoning every ounce of strength within me, I drive my knee into his groin, causing him to double over with a cry of pain.

"Fucking bitch," he groans.

I take my chance, clutching the glass shard the woman sent my way before I aim for his throat. It tears through his flesh with a sickening sound until blood gushes, and he splutters and gasps for air. He falls above me, hands clawing at my throat, and I fear he might kill me before he dies himself.

I'm choking as he restricts my flood of oxygen, but I hold out—feeling his grip loosening.

The Grimaldi made man collapses to the ground, life draining from his vacant eyes. He's dead, and I'm one step closer to taking them all down.

"There's a key in his pocket," the woman says, her voice not the least bit affected by the horrors that have transpired.

I swiftly search his pockets until my fingers close around the key. It slides smoothly into the lock of my chains, and with a satisfying click, the restraints fall away. I scramble to my feet, turning to the woman as I unlock her chains as well.

Wordlessly, we share a nod of understanding before springing into action, creeping toward the basement door in a desperate attempt to free ourselves. Adrenaline surges through me, making me unaware of the pain trying to sink me under the surface of lava.

But then, the door suddenly creaks open with an ominous sound that sends a chill down my spine. I freeze in place, seeing Peter Grimaldi standing before me, his eyes blazing with unleashed fury.

Behind him, his associates hinder any chance of escape, and panic surges through me. *He's supposed to be with the Ivanovas now.* I curse inwardly, feeling the first onslaught of pain searing through my battered body when they attack. Each blow is a cruel reminder of reality—how I got Viper back after years of believing he was dead, only to lose him again.

What I wouldn't do to be in his arms again...

I'm pushed to the ground, a sensation of lightning lashing across my already torn-up back as my resolve crumbles under despair.

In this very moment, I come to terms with my grim reality.

It's all fucking hopeless.

Chapter 20
Arcane

"MOVE IT, BITCH," THE voice behind me snarls, anger lacing his words as I turn to face the unknown woman.

Our eyes meet, and despite the impending doom approaching us, her gaze is comforting. We're being punished—I sense it down to my core as we're led out of the desolate basement room and into an unfamiliar blacksmith's shop, still inside the manor. The woman visibly swallows, her face gradually paling as if she's faced this ordeal before.

Tragedy hangs in the air, polluting it with its presence.

"Is it time to babysit us?" I snap at the associate leading us into the room, where two men await.

I try to struggle against his hold but, fuck, he's much taller than

I am, his strength overpowering my weakened body. With only one glass of water a day and enough food to keep me alive, I've been left starving for seven days.

The boundaries between reality and an illusion have started blurring together into a maddening haze, making me spiral into an abyss that seems endless. I guess that is what dehydration does to you—leaving you unable to think clearly, wallowing in your despair.

The walls I so carefully constructed around my soul over the past few years are gradually crumbling, revealing only the shell of who I am in the depths of this agony. I once believed everything would be okay again when the Valentis took me in and protected me like one of their own. I never thought they would be the ones to betray me, using me as leverage for power. Did my friendship with Alec mean nothing to him? I'm such a fool for ever trusting someone again.

I can do nothing when the man hooks the woman to the ceiling, her arms bound high, forcing her onto her tiptoes. Her eyes are vacant as if she tuned out reality and finds herself in a nonexistent world within her mind.

"I said, move it," the voice commands, shoving me until I tumble to the floor inside the blacksmith's chamber, knees thudding painfully against the surface.

I grit my teeth, anger boiling within me in waves, but I can't do anything with the three men inside the room, staring at me like predators closing in on their prey.

I look over at the woman, trying to find answers in her gaze, but she's unresponsive—slowly blinking, breathing, hinting that she's alive. But she's not here mentally. *Fuck this.*

The room is unlike any I've seen, intimidating with a forge and anvil in the middle, flanked by rows of tools and shelves. Stone walls enclose us, with a fireplace right beside the forge, casting shadows across the walls. A stone desk adorned with shackles sends my heart racing. What kind of place is this?

Beside the desk stands Peter Grimaldi, his posture relaxed yet authoritative, though he eyes the woman with equal parts lust and disgust. It sends shivers down my spine.

I wish I could end their pathetic lives like I killed their associate, but I have to bide my time, find the right moment to end their lives once and for all.

My knees go weak underneath me as I struggle to keep my balance when the two Grimaldi made men hoist me up, and it's not long before I'm guided toward the office desk. They force my chest down, their grip tightening around my arms.

I clench my fists, snarling at the men like a cornered beast, my muscles straining to get free yet knowing it's fucking pointless.

"Honestly, it was a mere coincidence you ended up with the Valentis. Didn't know about it until a year ago when they contacted me, wanting to make a business deal. You in exchange for territory and power," he spits out, venom dripping from his words.

"Where's Mom?" I ask him, interrupting him midway.

He clenches his fists out of frustration, grunting at me before saying with indifference, "I killed her."

Doesn't surprise me at all. She always was a weak fucker, never standing up for her foster children or herself. She tried so hard to fit into this criminal world, but you have to be a predator yourself to be able to live with one.

From the corner of my eye, I see the woman's interest pique, head tilting to the side as if tuning in on the conversation. It strikes me how little I know about her.

"After Kaiden died, you were worth nothing anymore. A pathetic, used slut. Don't you think I found out about the two of you? How you spread your legs for your brother like a whore? I could have gained so much from your virginity, but you just had to fuck your own brother."

His tirade thunders throughout the room, and I stare at him in disbelief. The rage is palpable in his tense muscles as if he's on the verge of exploding. Veins bulge in his temples, his face contorted into a mask of fury as his eyes burn with an intensity full of malice.

Meanwhile, my heart constricts with pain at hearing his words, like being hit by a train coming at full speed. Years of unanswered questions about why they threw me out finally gain clarity, and the truth cuts like knives into my chest. He meant to sell my body and my virginity. The mere thought makes me physically sick.

The mention of Kaiden's death makes that knife twist deeper, mingled with a sense of relief at the realization that Peter doesn't know about his survival.

A hidden smile hints on my lips that I quickly conceal when he scowls at me, a murderous glint in his eye. "I will mark you until there's nothing left of you to love. You were once beautiful, worth a fortune, but you won't be for much longer."

The woman closes her eyes, unnoticed by the other men, as she flinches slightly. I'm sure she's suffered through something like this during her month here, and she probably knows what's coming.

Peter turns around, retrieving an iron poker and thrusting it into the flames of the forge. He strikes the metal with the hammer, causing sparks to fly which reveals the heat of the glowing metal.

Panic grips me in its icy embrace when I intensify my struggles, but the two men overpower me, forcing me to be still as my foster father approaches with the searing iron poker, holding it so close to my face that sweat starts beading on my forehead.

"Stop!" I command, but my protests fall on deaf ears.

I instinctively lean away, but one of the men pushes my head closer to my father.

"This is going to hurt," he says while his lips stretch into a cruel smirk.

Then, a white-hot pain streaks across my cheek as he brands me with the heated iron. A primal scream rips from my throat at the agonizing brutality, tears gathering in my eyes that I refuse to let fall.

The pain is excruciating, burning and sizzling my flesh until my throat turns hoarse from the force of how loud I scream. The men chuckle sadistically, finding amusement in my misery. I'm on the brink of unconsciousness, my eyes drifting close as I desperately try to escape the unbearable reality.

This is where I die. At the hands of the man who once vowed to destroy my life when he realized I was useless. My heart caves in as I realize he's not only marked my soul but has now left a permanent scar on my skin, which will serve as a reminder of the man who ruined me.

The agony is so brutal that it threatens to consume me entirely, making me forget everything around me—the men, the woman, even the blacksmith's chamber. Minutes drag on in which I can't feel anything, lost in a fog of oblivion where only pain exists. Through the haze, I imagine hearing someone shout for me— Viper. But it's impossible. He can't be here, he will never find me, and I will never get the chance to tell him how much I hate and love him simultaneously—an obsession born from the depths of my shattered heart.

A hand muffles my cries, and I'm choking on air, fighting to breathe and scream, but everything blurs together as fatigue overwhelms me. I hear a whisper through the fog, so quiet I can barely make out what it is.

"Arcane."

Looking up, I find the image of a dangerously alluring man who once stole my heart years ago, never to return it. He stands in all his glory, a beacon of light in the darkness that slowly seeps into my soul. I know this is nothing more than an illusion.

There's no one left to save me now.

Blackness seeps into the edges of my vision, and a distant voice echoes in my ears, sounding like *his* voice. But it's too late. I'm lifted into someone's arms, pain and despair swirling within me, nausea churning as searing agony spreads through my cheek.

"Arcane, look at me," the voice pleads, but I resist, unwilling to face the harsh reality.

I don't want to see the destruction of what the Grimaldi men did to me—the scar they gave me. I certainly don't want to meet the eyes of the woman and see the pity in them, knowing I won't be able to handle it.

The dark, husky voice repeats itself, forcing me back to reality as someone's hand clamps around my throat. The touch is achingly familiar, causing a hurricane of emotions to surge within me. I force my eyes open and find myself staring into his—Viper's—eyes.

This time, he's not wearing a helmet or mask, showing his perfectly sculpted cheekbones and serious eyes. A subtle hint of worry lingers in his gaze beneath the expression of indifference, even though I know his true emotions that he's too terrified to show lurk just below the surface.

"Viper," I whisper, my voice barely audible amidst the chaos of my emotions.

The pain intensifies, but I summon the strength to meet his gaze, realizing that it's truly him and not a phantom of my imagination. Tears well in my eyes, and I despise feeling so vulnerable, but I'm so goddamn tired.

"You found me," I manage to stutter, voice quivering. I had my doubts that I'd never be found.

"I promised that I would always find you," he says, but his eyes harden when he looks at me, jaw clenching, a glint of something darker replacing the comfort. "What did they do to you?"

I'm unable to feel the weight of his gaze, so I turn away from him, hiding the ugly mark that mars my skin. Humiliation takes over rational thinking.

His finger hooks under my chin, wanting me to face him. With his other hand, he clamps his fingers around my throat, compelling me to meet his gaze. In those brown orbs, I feel lost and found all at once.

"Never hide from me, my devangel. This makes you no less beautiful. You're fucking stunning," he growls out with a possessive edge to his words, sending delicious tremors down my spine. Especially with how his hand tightens around my throat. "And you're still fucking mine."

With a solemn sigh, I want to avert my gaze from Viper again, overwhelmed by the intensity of his stare. But he refuses to let me escape—he has never truly allowed me to let go. My heart squeezes in my chest, torn between the fear of the unknown and future, and the strange sense of reassurance I feel at having him here.

I used to despise him for leaving me, for abandoning me in a man-made world while fighting to survive myself. But I've found that there's nowhere else I would rather be than with him, in whatever fucked-up state of mind he comes with—my fucking executor, my torturer, and my obsession.

In his eyes, I see flickers of flames and desire, revealing there's no escaping him, nor has there ever been. Even when he wasn't physically present, he was always there—watching over me, protecting me from the shadows, teasing and taunting me. He may lack the ability to feel emotions like others do—something I noticed when we were children—but he cares in his own fucked-up way.

His eyes convey all the things words alone cannot, binding me to him in ways I can't even begin to comprehend. He was the monstrous grave that shattered everything I once thought I was, yet since his return as Viper, he has been the force molding me into a stronger person who's no longer afraid of the world.

The muffled sounds around us shatter the moment, pulling me back to reality. Viper's gaze turns lethal as he glances over my shoulder, his eyes shifting to the men emerging from the shadows, armed and clad in uniform. I recognize them all from the meeting between the Garcías and the Valentis, the one I initially wasn't invited to. Among them, Peter Grimaldi kneels, bound and subdued by two imposing figures, while his closest men lie dead on the floor.

The unknown woman still hangs from the ceiling, her eyes meeting mine with a scrutiny I cannot place. She assesses me before casting a glare of distrust at Viper.

"Someone take her down," I demand, my tone sharp as I lock

eyes with Viper.

A burly man dressed in a snug uniform grunts in response before swiftly cutting down the chains that bind her. She falls to the floor with a dull thud that resonates in the tense atmosphere.

"Asshole," she mutters, and I can't help but smile at her.

There's something so unknown about her—she exudes mystery and loyalty, her presence commanding respect. I can't help but wonder where she comes from, but she hasn't revealed anything. She stands up, surveying the room with a stance suggesting she's ready to fight, an aura of distrust emanating from her. Her eyes eventually settle on mine, and I nod in acknowledgment.

"They're with me."

With a curt nod, she steps closer, leaning in to whisper something meant only for my ears.

"I'm Maven. Thank you," she murmurs, her gaze softening as she squeezes my shoulder—a gesture that speaks more than words.

Then, without another word, she's out of the manor, with no one stopping her as she leaves behind an air of mystery.

Confusion clouds my mind as I turn back to Viper. "How?" I manage to stutter, having a hard time understanding the turn of events, especially in the haze I'm still in.

He doesn't ask about the woman—I know he doesn't care what happens to her, so I rephrase my question. "How did you get here?"

Viper's lips curl into a cruel smirk, a mischievous glint swirling in his eyes. "They underestimated me." He chuckles darkly. "They let me go the moment they took you, not realizing who I was. I've been gathering all the Garcías to get you out of here. I'm sorry it took so long."

He pauses, hinting at his men to leave the room and give us privacy before ensuring I stare straight into his penetrating eyes.

"Understand, darling devil, that I've sought vengeance for us, for the childhood that was stolen from us. I've bided my time, waiting for you to fully embrace yourself, while rallying every García I could to help me. It's the only positive thing about being forced to take over." He sighs. "It's too bad that the opportunity arose after he'd already inflicted so much harm upon you." A hint of regret crosses his eyes. "We haven't been able to strike back before, but after you and the Valentis destroyed their weaponry that day, the Grimaldis were left vulnerable, distracted. They didn't even know we were coming."

A surge of emotions I can't put into words comes over me. Despite his usual detachment and lack of empathy for others, there's a part of him that's always cared about me.

"And the Valentis?" I ask, my voice betraying my emotions.

"Alec and his father are back at our home," he says, making sure to emphasize the word 'our' with a wink. "They're my gift to you, devil."

Despite the chaos and turmoil around us, a small smile tugs at the corners of my lips, revenge burning in my heart against those who have wronged me. This time, it's not Viper—it's the Valentis and the Grimaldis.

Viper's gaze shifts to our father on his knees behind us, his eyes glinting with a deadly intensity as he steps forward, fully revealing himself. I observe how our father's face drains of color, stuttering out incoherent words while seemingly pleading for his life.

"Hello, Daddy," Viper utters, tilting his head ever so slightly.

At that moment, despite the gravity of the situation, I can't help but notice how fucking hot Viper looks all murderous. Every line of his face is sharp, accentuated by the flickering shadows cast by the forge. Strands of his light hair fall across his forehead, tousled, adding to his rugged allure, and sweat glistens on his temples, revealing he fought his way inside the Grimaldi mansion.

Viper takes a step toward our father, a knife now in his hand, who stares at him with desperation and fear, pleading for his life, but he won't get any mercy at all. I witness Viper unleash all the pent-up rage and anguish from years of abuse, each strike of the knife in his hand a symbol of freedom.

"This is for Arcane," he declares, plunging the blade into our foster father's stomach, making him cry out in pain like a pathetic human being. "For how badly you treated her. For abandoning her when I was gone." Another slash, and the knife sinks into his leg. I observe his widened eyes, face paling further. "And this?" Viper's lips curl into a cruel smirk as he traces our father's throat, merely trailing it with the blade of the knife delicately above the fragile skin. "This is for me. For all the years of neglect and abuse at your hands." With a swift motion, he slices from left ear to right.

Blood splatters around the room, painting a vivid picture of our newfound freedom from the clutches of the Grimaldis.

When all is said and done, Viper looks at me, beautifully marked with blood, panting and heaving. Yet, a sense of tranquility comes over him, evident in how his shoulders visibly relax.

"Let's get out of here," I mumble, tired of the horrors staining the walls of this damned manor, permeated with memories of tragedy and betrayal.

He looks at me, brushing streaks of blond hair from his eye and managing to smear the blood on his forehead. "What about the drive? The underbelly?" he asks, searching my eyes for answers.

"Fuck that. Fuck them all. They can go to ruins, for all I care," I mutter, feeling the truth lacing my words.

It's true. I no longer give a fuck about the truce in this city. Penumbra Crest is tainted with blood and war, a place where people betray each other, and loyalties are scarce. And the people left? I couldn't care less if they died.

I stopped caring long ago when the thought of revenge took over all occupying thoughts.

"Let's start with ruining the Valentis," Viper looks at me with a glint of mischief in his eyes before turning to kiss me.

It's brutal, raw, and all the things that determine our relationship. Ours has never been a romance of candlelit dinners, gentle and passionate intimate moments. It's the kind that delves into the deeper edges, where our souls call to each other's darkness in ways no one would ever understand. The kiss carries poison, cloaked in sweetness to lure prey in before devouring, shared amidst the chaos of emotions and bloodshed.

Destruction looms over us, but *oh*, it has never felt more bittersweet.

Epilogue
Arcane

THE NIGHT SKY LOOMS ominously overhead, a foreboding shadow casting over the sinister mansion. But unlike all those years ago, I've escaped the clutches of the Grimaldis once and for all. Back then, I underestimated the evil of this world. Things have changed.

I have changed.

If someone had told me Kaiden would resurface after years of his supposed death, I'd never believe them. They declared he died in a train wreck shortly after midnight on my twenty-first birthday, the tenth of July. Yet, I should have known better. While they claimed he was dead, no body was ever discovered, despite the media's relentless pursuit.

That's the thing about a town where criminals reign—there's corruption seeping into every crevice.

With our foster father gone and the Valentis soon to follow, chaos looms over Penumbra Crest. It's no longer my burden. This town has failed me repeatedly, leaving me with little to offer except my allegiance to Viper as we navigate our uncertain future.

With each heartbeat, anticipation thrums through me, heightening my senses as I clench the handle tighter. The knife becomes a comfort as I inhale deeply, waiting for the long-awaited end after years of seeking vengeance.

Agonizing screams from the basement shatter through the silence of the manor, enveloping us all with their horrors. I glance at Viper, his stance relaxed with a concealed smirk betraying his sinister intentions, allowing me to soak in the unfolding scene before us.

It's tragically beautiful in its own macabre way, with two men hanging from the ceiling, their muffled cries slicing through the air like haunting music. I never imagined finding pleasure in their agony, nor did I foresee stepping foot inside the García mansion. Now, it's my stage for revenge.

Despite my attempts to fit into the Valenti organization, I never truly was one of them, was I?

A deep sigh of irritation follows as I suppress the feeling of self-pity, allowing a festering rage to take its hold, burning and brimming with the need for an outlet.

With my wounds throbbing and days of torture weighing on

me, I press on, fueled by determination. Viper promised me a gift, and this is where he brought me after we left the Grimaldi mansion.

"They're my gift to you, devil."

Viper was right. As soon as I descended into the basement, the stench of urine, sweat, and blood assaulted me—fear and suffering. Now, with the knife in hand and Viper pressed taut against my back, I stand ready to exact the revenge that's rightfully mine.

With icy resolve, I step forward, confronting Benjamin Valenti. Seeing him vulnerable is oddly refreshing, a testament to Viper's effort to ensure his and his son's capture, gifting me their lives.

Viper is shirtless behind me, his mouth peppering kisses along my neck, nibbling my lobe.

"Do whatever you wish with them," he whispers, his words laden with sensuality.

As his hands skate lower, from my shoulder to my breasts, playing with the straps of my bra underneath the T-shirt, I attempt to resist the intoxicating touch, but in truth, I'm nervous to face the Valentis after what has transpired.

I let Viper's hands glide off my body and strike Benjamin's cheek, leaving a red mark. He stirs awake with swollen eyes— courtesy of Viper—and directs a sneer of disdain toward me. I tear away the fabric gagging both him and Alec, meant to silence them.

"Fuck you," he spits out, snot running down his nose.

Rage surges through me at his audacity to insult me, when I hold the upper hand for once.

"That wasn't very nice," I remark with a smile, taunting him, just before plunging the blade into Benjamin's thigh.

It sinks into his flesh with a sickening squelch, causing him to scream out in agony, louder this time with the gag gone. Oh, it feels euphoric to inflict pain, remembering all the times he looked down on me.

"You're pathetic," I sneer at him, noticing the sweat clinging to his forehead, his face dirty and swollen.

Viper's touch traces over my figure from behind, sending shivers cascading across my fragile skin. I lean into his touch. His roughened fingertips explore my chest, grazing beneath the T-shirt he loaned me, then finding my nipples with purpose.

I can't help but enjoy it, allowing it to become my anchor of safety while reveling in the comfort.

"They can look all they want, but as long as they so much as *see* you, they're as good as dead." Viper whispers the words like a teasing caress.

The two Valentis won't live to see another day. Their fate was sealed the moment they laid eyes on me while Viper's touch lingered on me.

"A-Arcane, please don't do this. We're f-family," Alec stutters, eyes wide and face pale. He looks far from the composed man I've known him to be.

"Alec, shut the fuck up," his father snaps, and I tsk at them both.

"Family?" I scoff. "Apparently, we never were family. You betrayed me. Why?"

The question isn't one from a place of emotion or sorrow, it's fueled purely by curiosity and the need to understand why it was so important to ruin our friendship.

A look of regret flashes across his eyes, yet I remain unaffected. He betrayed me. He knew about all the anxiety I felt growing up because I confided in him. We were supposed to be best friends, but he never once stood up for me when the men around us disregarded me for simply being a woman.

As Viper kneads my nipples, a gasp escapes my throat. His hand trails lower, the feeling intoxicating and unforgettable. It descends until his finger skims the edge of my underwear.

"You're right. You never were a part of our family." Benjamin Valenti spits on the floor before me. I turn to him, fists clenched, annoyance etched across my face. "It was so easy to trick you into believing you were one of us."

I twist the knife still lodged in his thigh, relishing the agony flickering in his face, though he tries to conceal it. Even though I have demanded answers for their betrayal, I already know the truth from Peter Grimaldi. "It's the Grimaldis, isn't it?"

An amused glint replaces the agony, and Benjamin flashes a crooked grin. "Yes. And soon our allies will be here, ruining everything you think you've accomplished."

He casts an unreadable expression toward Viper, and I follow his gaze, seeing Viper before me with a predatory gleam in his eyes. Satisfaction is palpable in the air when his touch slips underneath my panties. I can't help but clench my thighs, all the while maintaining eye contact with Benjamin.

"I wonder how that's supposed to happen."

Viper kisses my neck, a low hum emanating from his throat. "It's sure to be impossible when they're all dead."

My eyes shift from Benjamin to Alec, who appears nauseous, trying not to glance at where Viper's hand rests.

"That's right," I reply with a cruel smirk.

Alec's gaze drifts up to the ceiling, his head heavy with exhaustion in those tired, pale eyes.

"Now you know how it feels," I tell him, voice tinged with anger. "When you decided power and territory were more important than found family. When you lied to me and pretended to be on my side, all the while planning for the Grimaldis to have me."

He continues to stare at the ceiling, his Adam's apple bobbing as he nervously swallows.

"Fucking look at me!" I scream, and he flinches, finally meeting my gaze. "You should know by now that I don't take kindly to those who betray me. Peter Grimaldi is already dead, and now, so will you."

"Please," he stutters, but I see the truth in his eyes. The regret he previously showed isn't because he regrets betraying me for power; it's because he lost a friend for entirely selfish reasons.

"You're going to pay for what you did to me," I hiss, my voice dripping with venom.

The façade of regret Alec wore while feigning innocence slips away, revealing a cold, calculated look. It's unsettling to see him so out of character, but I realize now that this is the true him.

"You're ruining everything," he seethes. "All of our plans." This time, he doesn't avert his gaze.

I swallow, hiding my shock at his words, but Viper's hand, as it trails inside my panties, tapping on my clit, brings me back to the present.

I wrench the knife from Benjamin's thigh, driving it into Alec's stomach instead, coating the blade in blood. He bites his tongue hard, staring at me with hatred so deep it nearly makes me recoil.

"Fucking bitch. A woman doesn't belong in this world of criminality."

I feel no remorse for my actions, tired of being underestimated by misogynistic men. Instead, I plunge the knife straight into Alec's heart as his impending fate dawns upon him. A strangled gasp escapes him, his scream of rage and agony echoing off the walls. He's not sorry for hurting me. He's sorry for what *he* lost, the chances he wasted.

It's painful to witness Alec's body convulsing against the chains around his wrists, the blade gradually piercing his heart. I know there's no other choice if I want to earn my freedom. He desperately tries to fight the inevitable, his eyes meeting mine with betrayal seeping into his bones—it feels as if he's the one twisting the weapon in me. A lone tear trickles down my cheek.

"You shouldn't have betrayed me. I'm sorry." I look away like a coward as my once best friend takes his last breath, blood gushing from the wound and dripping onto the floor.

"Shh, don't worry, devangel," Viper whispers soothingly, his finger finding my folds and pushing inside me.

It's erotically fucked up, with the heartache of my supposed best friend's corpse in the background.

Meanwhile, Benjamin Valenti screams incomprehensibly. There's not an ounce of sadness in his eyes, as if Alec's life means nothing to him.

"I'll never bend to you again." I curse at Benjamin, tightening my grip around the blade, its edge tearing through his throat next.

There's resistance, but it yields to the force, all the while knowing Viper is behind me and has my back. Benjamin's blood spurts out, creating a gruesome scene.

Never once does Viper attempt to seize control and take over my act of revenge, allowing me to pursue it for myself. He has never treated me like I'm less than for being a woman. Instead, he empowers me *because* of it. He doesn't try to change me or my ways, he simply exists in the background as a support for when I need him, and for that I'll forever be grateful.

I will never bend for a man who doesn't treat me with respect ever again.

The basement is a grim mess of death and decay, yet as Viper turns me around, ripping his shirt off my torso, it has never felt more like freedom.

"I told you, you're as exquisite as a blood angel from hell."

His smirk widens, revealing perfect teeth as he takes me in, and I do the same, noticing how bloody I've become. He leans closer, licking the blood that sprayed over my neck, sucking on my skin.

"Delicious," he says.

"You're psychotic."

"Call it what you want, darling. It takes one to know one."

He winks before his fingers move in and out of me, and I can't help but gasp.

Tension crackles in the air between us, charged with electricity, as he leans in and captures my lips. Lust overwhelms me when he suddenly grabs the bloodied knife from my hand, using it to cut through the fabric of my panties, leaving me all naked and vulnerable amidst the chaos around us. Alec's and Benjamin's lifeless bodies still hang from the ceiling, and Viper cuts them down.

The next thing I know, he binds me to the ceiling, his hardness pressing against my backside. He growls, and my heart races as I struggle against the restraints. Fear and excitement mingle in me, making me breathless as desire pools between my legs, wetness trickling down my thighs.

"What are you doing?" I manage to breathe out.

He merely chuckles, the sound grating on my nerves, sending shivers down my spine.

I hear the unmistakable sound of his belt unbuckling, dragging his hand over my naked body, painting it like a canvas with the blood of those who betrayed me. Viper teases my entrance with his two piercings, his breaths uneven as I'm forced to stand on my tiptoes, blood pooling beneath me on the floor. My bare feet are drenched.

It's a mixture of wrong and fucked up, but I can't seem to find it in me to care. Fuck them all.

Without another second to spare, he thrusts into me, evoking a scream of pleasure as I clench around him.

"Hmm, I wonder what happens if I do this…" he muses, retrieving lube from his pocket—he planned this, no doubt. I watch as he slathers the knife's handle with lubricant before lining it up against my ass.

"Breathe for me," he whispers in my ear, letting me feel the handle of the knife. "Relax, my little sinful angel."

I do, and he gently guides it inside my ass, causing a guttural moan as my eyes roll back in ecstasy. He holds the handle there, the knife's blade cutting into his hand, adding slickness as he continues to drive into me. Harder and faster, until I'm screaming his name, surrounded by the gore around us. He fucks me in a brutal way that shows his emotions in the only way he can.

"Are you *attempting* to make me come with the thought of my brother's cum dripping from my legs?" I tease him, and he growls, squeezing my neck with his free hand to assert dominance and intensify his thrusts.

"I'm not attempting to do anything. I'm fucking succeeding,

and you're loving every second of it, you dripping, gorgeous slut."

My air is cut off as my inner walls clench around his pierced length, waves of pleasure shooting through me. My wrists throb from days of torment and captivity, yet I realize now that this is his way of helping me heal—replacing the bad memories with new, better ones.

He drives me to the point of climax until he finds release, too, grunting out my name like a prayer meant for the devil. I'm breathless as he withdraws, his cum trickling down my leg in a forbidden cascade. He easily unties my wrists, steadying my body to prevent me from slipping on the blood before ensuring our eyes lock.

It feels as if a vise squeezes my heart with the words lingering on the tip of my tongue, demanding to be released no matter the consequences. Without allowing him to say anything, I lay my heart bare.

"I-I think I love you," I confess, the words tumbling out hesitantly.

He stiffens as if grappling with disbelief. It takes him a moment to respond. The short laugh escaping him is one I didn't expect.

"No one can love me," he states matter-of-factly, yet his eyes betray a vulnerability, a doubt about what love truly means. Neither of us is familiar with such emotions.

"I've fallen for you," I insist, and he hesitates, searching my eyes for the truth in my words.

And I know that even if he doesn't say it back, he feels it too, in his own twisted way.

"I can't give you a fairy tale. I'm not the kind to shower you with chocolates and flowers," he begins, and I'm about to protest, confusion knitting my brows. "I can't say I love you because I don't even know what love is."

He pauses, letting his words sink in. My heart beats rapidly inside my rib cage, nerves eating me from the inside.

"But what I can give you is forever because I'm so goddamned obsessed with you," he finishes with a loud sigh.

His gaze pierces mine, and a swell of emotions threatens to overwhelm me. It's the closest thing to affection he can offer, and strangely, I'm okay with that. Because not everyone can feel love, but that doesn't mean they don't deserve to be loved.

"Then take me. Forever. I'm yours," I declare, admitting it out loud, fully aware of the gravity of my words.

I never wanted to admit it as a young adult, but deep down, I guess I've always known there's no escaping him. And truthfully, I don't want to.

He smiles, a beautiful one that shatters the barriers around my heart, leaving me utterly exposed.

As he takes in the scene around us—two bodies strewn about, blood pooling, and the clock striking midnight—he leans in close to my ears.

"Happy birthday, Arcane," he whispers, words laced with emotions I never imagined I'd hear from him.

―――――――――

FIVE YEARS AGO, YOU saved me from the streets, offering me a friendship I never thought I'd find again. I will forever be grateful for that. You were there when I needed a shoulder to lean on, but in the end, it wasn't enough. I forgive you for your betrayal, even though it stings. I know I won't truly move on until I find forgiveness within myself.

May you rest in peace wherever you are, and find the comfort your soul always craved.

I'm sorry for how it all turned out. I miss you, Alec, but I hope you understand why I did what I did. After all, all I've ever done is fight to survive.

A xx

Ripping the paper into shreds, I release it to the wind, watching as it scatters over the cliff's edge and into the water. With each piece carried away by a strong gust of wind, a weight lifts from my shoulders, and I bury the last pit of anxiety within.

A farewell to the best friend I lost.

I look up at the rumbling sky, enjoying the turbulent storm on its way to Penumbra Crest with the chaos looming closer. The entire town is corrupting, falling apart, but I don't care.

Standing from my spot, I turn to face the man leaning against the sleek black R1 bike, his form covered in a leather jacket and gloves. His helmet rests on the seat, his hair tousled by the wind.

There's an enigmatic expression on his face that sets butterflies slicing my stomach.

Our relationship may not fit the standards, but it's our reality. I meet his gaze, realizing he's the only thing that truly matters now.

With a smile dancing on my lips, I feel the glistening droplets of rain fall from above. I make my way over to him, meeting his gaze with an intensity that crackles the air around us.

"No one will ever hurt you again," he promises, as if reading my thoughts and the unspoken pain in my heart.

His lips crash against mine, a dangerous blend of poison and desire that leaves me craving more. As he hands me my helmet, I mount my own bike parked beside his.

"Thank you," I tell him, acknowledging everything he's done for me—even the fucked-up parts that shaped me into the strong woman I've become.

He nods, his jaw clenched tight. A mischievous expression plays on his face as he meets my gaze, his eyes smoldering with desire and promises to come.

"Now, drive before I catch you."

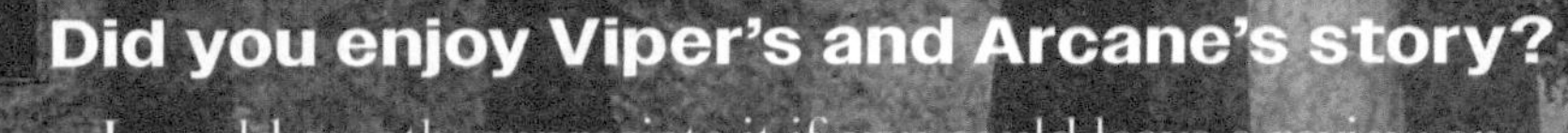

Did you enjoy Viper's and Arcane's story?

I would greatly appreciate it if you could leave a review on Amazon and Goodreads. Your thoughts and reviews make a huge difference. Thank you for your support!

ALSO BY RAINELYN

Tainted Souls Trilogy
Ethereally Tainted
Tainted Serenity

Standalones
His Doll
Monstrous Grave

ACKNOWLEDGEMENTS

While this book may or may not have been a quick read, it was primarily crafted for the enjoyment of dark, smut romance enthusiasts, yet it holds a special place in my heart. Arcane's journey embodies themes of loss and sorrow transforming into a quest for vengeance. Her story reflects a woman navigating a world shaped by men, reminiscent of historical societal norms, where she initially strives to conform but ultimately discovers that she doesn't need to adhere to society's morals.

I wrote this book for everyone who feels lost from time to time, and who doesn't believe they fit into society. You're always loved, and you're perfect just the way you are.

Thank you to every single person on my team who has helped shape this book into what it is today. Misha, Rumi, Lindsey — you are all stars who have made this journey so much smoother while I poured my heart and soul into delivering the book I am so passionate about.

Special thanks to Unalive Promotions for their invaluable support in promoting and releasing Monstrous Grave.

Elijah, you're an amazing friend who deserves all the love in the world. Your unwavering support, love, and feedback have been incredibly meaningful, and I count myself lucky to have gotten to know you. You claimed this book from the very beginning, so this is for you xx Love you!

Finally, thank you to my readers for sticking with me through everything. To everyone who promoted my book, applied for an ARC, bought a copy, and supported me, your encouragement means the world to me. I never dreamed my books would resonate with people as they have, and it's truly a dream come true.

I hope you enjoyed this journey, and remember, never let anyone dictate your worth. Stay true to yourself—you're fucking awesome.

All my love,

Rainelyn xx

ABOUT THE AUTHOR

Rainelyn is an independent author whose books explore themes of darkness and gothic, as well as troubled characters and their unusual love stories. With her writing style and twisted stories, she is well known for making her readers' hearts swell with all the emotions and imagery she evokes in her books.

She loves to write anything that involves steam, danger, depraved darkness, and morally ambiguous characters that ride the line between good and evil.

When she's not writing, she enjoys cuddling with her dog and partner, aka her real-life book boyfriend. She is a sucker for gaming, listening to music, and creating new book adventures.

Feel free to reach out to her on social media, Rainelyn loves to hear from her readers.

Want to stalk her on social media?

Instagram: @authorrainelyn

Facebook: @authorrainelyn

TikTok: @authorrainelyn

To find all her links, including Newsletter, Website:

www.ingramcontent.com/pod-product-compliance
Lightning Source LLC
LaVergne TN
LVHW041502170726
843492LV00005B/1340